T0114557

OK, I'm a Christian, NOW WHAT?

Debbie J. Libbey

The people and the story in this book are all fictional, but the biblical truths are not.

WestBow Press books may be ordered through booksellers or by contacting:

WestBow Press
A Division of Thomas Nelson & Zondervan
1663 Liberty Drive
Bloomington, IN 47403
www.westbowpress.com
1 (866) 928-1240

ISBN: 978-1-5127-3973-2 (sc)
ISBN: 978-1-5127-3974-9 (e)

Print information available on the last page.

WestBow Press rev. date: 04/28/2016

This book is dedicated
To
My Husband Charles Libbey
Thank you for letting me
Monopolize the computer.
And
To my boss and friend
Vallerie Harvey
Who inspired me to get this book published

My friend, I want to state that if you are content with your church and happy with your life. I'm not out to change you or try to tell you that you are right or wrong. If you are happy, then I believe you are right where you belong. But if you are questioning your church or where you are at spiritually, then my hope is that this book will help answer some questions, or even stir up some questions you hadn't thought of before. Either way I love you and rejoice with your growth.

I think of this book as a seed being scattered in the field. I know some seeds will fall on rocks and quickly be washed away (hated even). Some will fall on shallow ground where it will be acknowledged as truth but because of tradition, will not take root. I can only pray that a few seeds will fall on accepting soil, take root and grow. I pray you will be that one where the biblical truths of this book can flourish.

-1-

Becky walks slowly home from church on this warm Sunday afternoon. She had turned down the ride home from the nice couple from church. She needs some time to think. She takes the back roads to avoid the traffic, even though it is a longer route. It is quieter and it gives her the time she needs to think. Her mind wanders. *Who am I? How did I get here? Where am I going?*

She thinks back over her life. She is an only child. Kind of average, neither outgoing nor shy. Her parents are good people, not religious, she never remembered going to church, but they taught her right from wrong as best they could, and she loves them. She is happy that they live in the same town, though she doesn't see them or talk to them much. Since they retired and got that RV they are gone more than they are home. In High school she went though her rebellious stage and ran with the wrong crowd. She went for the "bad boys". It was fun and exciting but the minute she said "no" to anything, whether it was, stealing or sex or drugs or giving them money or whatever, the guy of her dreams would dump her for someone who would say "yes". After getting her heart broken not once but three times, she gave up on boys and the "Bad" life and started knuckling down and studying. She graduated with a B average and went to college.

Now at 25 she has a job as an administrative assistant. The pay's not great but it pays the bills. She has an apartment with a roommate, Jenifer. Her life seems to be on track but she seems to feel empty inside, that is, until two months ago when she went to a traveling church revival meeting with a friend of a friend and ended up giving her life to Christ. At that moment everything changed in her. She found peace and happiness unlike anything she had ever known before. Like a hole in her soul had been filled. She tried to explain it to her parents and her roommate but was meet with criticism. Her parents told her, "That's nice honey. We are glad for you, but Church and that whole 'religion' thing just isn't for us. We worship God in our own private way."

Her roommate thinks she is totally crazy and has given her an ultimatum, "Stop this nonsense or I am going to move out". When Becky doesn't change back to her old self. Jenifer decides to move. Becky thinks she can manage on her own but it will be tight. It also means she will have to get a car since Jenifer is taking their only car. Ok, it is her car but they both use it. Becky doesn't feel bad or resentful about losing her roommate. It is probably for the best. They haven't been getting along well lately and since she became a Christian, things have gotten worse. Jenifer argues about everything and blames it on Becky being a Christian. Becky is beginning to think Jennifer is possessed or something. Anyway Jenifer is moving out today and Becky isn't in a hurry to get home.

As she walks, her thoughts move to a different subject, Church. She has been a Christian for two months, that's about eight Sundays, and she has gone to almost as many different churches trying to find the "right one", the one that will answer her questions. Starting with the first one, she was told she is a sinner and that she needs to repent, so she did but she is unsure just what sin is.

The first church tells her, "Sin is anything your conscience says it is and that can be different for each person." That may be partly true, but Becky can't quite buy that that is all there is to it. So she tries the next church.

She is told, "You just have to do what our 'Leader' tells you to do. He will take control of your whole life. He will tell you your every move. Just do what he says and you won't have to worry about anything."

Becky reluctantly says, "Ok, … so when do I get to meet him?"

Sister Sara tells her, "Oh, you can't meet him. You can't even talk to him. He just tells you what to do and what not to do."

Becky asks, "But he doesn't even know me. How can he tell me what to do?"

"Oh, he just knows. He has a direct line to God," Sara says.

"HE does?" Becky asks with suspicion, "and I don't?"

"Oh no, you can talk to God, but God only talks back to 'the Leader'. We can only listen to what 'our leader' says, then do it," she replies.

"So you just blindly follow a man? What if he's wrong?" asks Becky.

"He is never wrong. He can't be wrong. He is God's one and only. Our Leader," the "sister" tells her with all sincerity.

Becky thanks the girl and leaves.

Becky isn't about to give her life over to a "man" she never even gets to meet. She instinctively knows that isn't right. She worships God, not a man.

The next church just seems to repeat the same thing every week, "Repent and give your life to Jesus". Becky thinks, "O*k, I did that, now what*?" But when she tries to talk to the pastor (a man much older then she is), his wife comes barging in and accuses them of having an affair. The pastor tries to calm her down and explain that he is just counseling her but the lady isn't buying it. She is yelling, "IF SHE NEEDS COUNSELING. LET HER TALK TO HER HUSBAND OR THE OLDER WOMEN IN THE CHURCH. SHE DOESN'T HAVE TO 'TALK' TO YOU." The woman is ranting. Becky leaves that church as fast as she can.

Then there was that church that she had to "interview" with first, before she could even go to their church to see if she was "good enough" for them. That should have been a red flag right there, but she went through with the first telephone interview anyway. The Lady, a Ms. White, snootily asks, "so describe yourself to me."

"Ok, I'm a white female. I'm 25 years old, and single. I'm 5 feet 8 inches tall, not too fat or too thin. I have short curly medium brown hair. I go to the gym three times a week after work with my roommate Jenifer. I have a full time job at a small business in town as a secretary, I mean administrative assistant. I accepted Christ as my personal savior a month and a half ago at a traveling revival meeting and have been looking for a church ever since," Becky says.

Ms. White then asks, "Are you baptized?"

Becky answers, "No, I didn't know I had to be baptized. What… exactly… is that?"

"You don't know about baptism? Well it's where you go under water in the name of the Father, Son and Holy Ghost in repentance of sin. You really should look it up.

"You do own a bible don't you?" Ms. White asks, getting more self righteous with every question.

"Yes, Ma'am, I own a bible," Becky answers a bit huffily.

Ms. White says, "Well, dear, I don't think you are right for our church at this time. I can set up counseling and training for you, if you are still interested in joining our church. Classes have already started for this quarter. Our next class starts in three months. Do you want me to sign you up?"

"No, that won't be necessary," Becky says, and hangs up. She thinks, "t*hat was a waste of time. But I should look into that Baptism thing though."*

This last church seems ok, but she still isn't getting any answers. It's all like cotton candy. Very sweet, but just a bunch of fluff and air and not a lot of scriptures to back up what is said. She shakes her head then prays this prayer, "Dear God, please help me find the right church for me. In Jesus' name. Amen."

-2-

She walks on and sees a man about her age trying to pull up a bush in the front yard of a house. He is nice looking, Becky thinks, not that she is looking for a boyfriend. He is probably married. All the good ones are, but she is drawn to help him anyway. So she goes over and helps pull the bush out.

He says, "Thank you, my name is Tom. I am the Pastor of this church."

Becky smiles and says, "Hi, Pastor Tom, my name is Becky. Glad to meet you." They shake hands.

"Happy to meet you too. So, are you ready to tackle the next bush?" Becky just looks at him. Tom snaps out of his "clearing bushes" mode and says "Oh… you're wearing nice clothes. I guess I can't ask you to get your Sunday clothes all dirty."

Becky says, " It's not that I don't want to help, if I was wearing my old clothes but I am confused. What kind of church is this? It looks like a regular house to me."

Tom smiles a smile that makes Becky's heart melt. She feels more at home than she has felt in a long time. She feels like she can ask this man anything, like he is a long lost friend.

"This is what is called a home church. We believe in the Biblical Sabbath. Which means we go to church on Saturday.

Thus the name of this church is 'The Lord of the Sabbath church,'" Tom says.

Becky looks at him bewildered. Tom continues, "You look like you have a lot of questions that I would love to answer, but right now I have to get these dead bushes out of here. I have a regular job I go to Monday thru Friday. I'm a male nurse over at the Doctors Clinic, and three nights a week I volunteer at the free clinic downtown. Sunday is the only day I can work on this yard. So unless you can help, you will have to make an appointment for later."

"Impressive, I do want to help," Becky says, "but..." and looks down at her clothes again.

"If you really want to help, I think we have some old overalls you can put on. You can either put them on over your clothes, or you can go inside and change," Tom says hopefully.

Becky says brightly, "Ok, where can I change?"

Tom smiles again, "Great, I really can use the help. Follow me." He goes in the house and finds the overalls then shows Becky where the restroom is. "I'll be outside, just come on out when you are ready." He goes back outside. In a few minutes Becky joins him, wearing the too large and baggy overalls that she is wearing over her own clothes. Tom has to stifle a laugh when he sees her. He decides he rather likes this girl that came from nowhere. He thinks they can be friends. Together they pull up weeds and dead bushes. They mark off the driveway with white stones. Then they till and fertilize the yard and flower bed, and plant grass seed. Tom stands up and says "Wow, I could not have gotten all this done without you". Just then his stomach growls loudly. "I think my stomach is trying to tell me something, like I'm hungry. Shall we get some lunch?"

Becky looks at her watch and says, "More like supper time now."

Tom looks at his watch and says, "Wow, I didn't realize how late it is. I hope your husband or boyfriend won't be mad at me for keeping you so long?"

At that Becky has to smile. "No worries, I don't have either."

"Oh…So how does a really cute girl like you not have at least a boyfriend?" Tom asks sincerely.

Becky, looking a little embarrassed, says, "I don't know, just haven't found the right guy, I guess. Haven't been looking for him either, I must confess."

"Why's that?' Tom asks.

"More important things on my list of must-dos, and, no, I'm not gay, if that's what you're thinking," Becky adds.

"The thought never crossed my mind," Tom genuinely says.

"What about you? Are you married or anything?" Becky asks.

"Me? Nope, no girls in my life except my mom. She lives in the next state over," Tom replies. "Not gay either," he throws in just to be clear.

"Good," Becky sighs, "I don't want to go through that again."

"Go through what again?" Tom asks as they both head to the kitchen in the house to find some food.

Becky explains, "I went to ask a pastor some questions. All very innocent but his crazy wife barged in and started accusing me of sleeping with her husband. I mean really the guy was old enough to be my father and I just met him. I'm not that kind of girl."

"So what did you do?" Tom inquired.

"I did what any girl would do. I left and never went back. Besides I doubt he would have answered my question anyway," Becky sighs, " I'm beginning to think no one can, or will."

"So what's your question?" Tom asks as he sets a sandwich and a cold bottle of water down in front of Becky.

Becky drinks down half the bottle and takes a bite of her cheese sandwich. "This is good, thanks, I didn't realize how hungry and thirsty I was."

"Yeah, me neither," Tom says as he too wolfs down a sandwich and goes for a second. "Your question?" Tom looks at her intently.

"I just want to know, 'What is sin?' I became a Christian a couple of months ago and have been going from church to church trying to find out that simple question. I know the Bible says 'All have sinned and come short of the glory of God' and that 'no man can come to God except through Jesus, and that we are to repent and sin no more'. I've done the first part of that, but how can I not sin, if I don't know what sin is?"

"That's a good question," Tom says, "Let me get my Bible and let's see what it says. Here it is, in. **1 John 3:4 KJV - 4 Whosoever commits sin transgresses also the law: for sin is the transgression of the law**. Or another translation says,

"Whoever commits sin also commits lawlessness, for sin is acting like there is no law."

Becky thinks about this for a moment then asks, "What law?"

"That would be the Law of God," Tom says with a twinkle in his eye.

"So what is the Law of God?" Becky is intrigued.

"That is of course the million dollar question now, isn't it?" Tom smiles and continues, "there are reportedly 613 Biblical Laws in the Old Testament alone, but I think we should start with what Jesus said in the new testament first. Except it's getting late. Can we take this up next week? It's dark outside. Can I give you a lift home?"

"I don't live far from here but… sure," Becky tells Tom. They walk outside and get into Tom's old car. It coughs and comes to life as he turns the key. They drive to her apartment building' which isn't far away at all. "This is fine. I'll get out here," she tells Tom when they get close to her apartment.

"Ok I'll see you next week then," Tom says, "and you can return the overalls then."

Becky looks down and sees that she forgot to take off the overalls. "Oh, oops," Becky says and they both laugh. She starts to leave, then abruptly turns back and asks.

"What time?" Tom looks at her and she adds, "Church on Saturday right? What time does it start?"

"Oh, yes, Saturday the main service starts at 2 pm." Tom says. He starts to say something more, but Becky unwittingly cuts him off.

"OK, I'll be there. What should I wear? I've found some churches want you to dress in your best and some just come in whatever," Becky inquires, as she looks down at the oversized overalls she has on.

"Well, we aren't the fashion police, but at the same time you are going there to be with Jesus and God, the King of Kings. So I guess you decide. Do you want me to come pick you up?" Tom asks.

"No, I think I'll walk. But thank you for asking," Becky smiles.

"Do you remember the way? Or should I give you the address?" Tom asks.

"I think I remember," she says, a bit sarcastically. "but just in case, give me the address anyway, please," Becky says trying to look innocent and kind-of flirty at the same time.

Tom gives Becky the church's card with the address and phone number on it, but before he gives it to her, he writes down his cell phone number. "If you need anything call me, Ok?"

"Ok," Becky promises. As she gets out of his car. She watches as he pulls away, after she shows Tom her house key so he knows she can get into her apartment. She smiles as she goes to her now empty apartment. Except for the furniture that belongs in the semi furnished two bedroom apartment and her own meager belongings, the place has been emptied out. She had forgotten how many of the things in the apartment were Jenifer's and how little she actually owns. "*Tomorrow I will have to see if I can get a cheaper one bedroom apartment. I don't need a two bedroom place anymore.*" She has no intention of getting another roommate, at least not any time soon. She feels free, like a weight has been lifted from her shoulders, but at the same time it does seem very quiet and a little lonely. "Maybe I'll get a cat or at least a TV," she says to the walls. She picks up her pillow and tells it, "I think

I'm going to like this weird home church. The Pastor sure is nice, but I like the other more traditional Sunday church too. Oh, pillow, what am I going to do?" A thought comes into her mind, or is it the pillow talking? It says, "*Pray and ask God for wisdom. He will tell you what to do.*" A Bible quote comes to mind. *'Prove all things whether they be right or wrong.'* Or something like that. "I need to read my Bible more, learn where things are, and what it actually says, and stop taking what other people say is in it as fact. I need to prove it for myself. That's what I like about Tom. He doesn't just tell me what the Bible says, he shows me. And I need to stop talking to pillows." She giggles and puts the pillow down.

She remembers she needs a ride to work tomorrow and calls her best friend and coworker, Lisa, to see if she can give her a ride. Lisa says, "Ok, I'll see you tomorrow." And hangs up. Becky smiles and gets ready for bed but not before asking God to help her know which church is right for her.

-3-

Monday morning Lisa is at Becky's place right on time. The two women greet each other as Becky gets in Lisa's car. It's a small car and a bit tight for Becky's liking, not that she isn't grateful for the ride. She is. She is just trying to figure out what kind of car she wants to get. She knows she doesn't want a big gas guzzler, but she's not fond of the tiny compacts like Lisa's car either. Something in the middle, she guesses. After work Lisa takes Becky to a good used car dealer.

"I can vouch for this place." Lisa tells her, "They have good cars for a fair price. It's where I got my little car 'Ruby'. I love her, she is very dependable. You can't go wrong with a Toyota. I've heard Hondas are good too. Do you want me to hang around? I will if you need me to, but I really need to get home."

"No, I'm sure I'll find something here. You go on. I'll be fine. If I need a ride home I have someone I can call," Becky tells Lisa, "Thank you for everything. I owe you one. I'll see you in the morning."

"Ok, if you're sure," Lisa says.

"Yes. Now go, I'll be fine, and thank you again," Becky says as she shuts the car door.

Lisa yells out, "No problem," as she drives away.

Becky turns around to find a salesman standing ready to help her. He holds out his hand and says, "Hi, I'm William, welcome to Bobs used cars. How can I help you today?"

"Hi, I'm Becky, I'm looking for an inexpensive midsized car."

"Sure, I can help you with that. We have some midsized ones right over here." As William leads Becky to the middle of the lot. "We have three nice cars right here, and if you don't see what you want, I believe we have some more in the back."

Becky looks them over and asks if she can test drive the gold colored Dodge Dart on the end.

"Sure," William says, " I'll go get the key. Be right back."

Becky looks at the car. She picked this one mostly because it was the cheapest of the three. But also she likes the look of it. The previous owner had glued a two inch high letter P on the side of the roof next to the back window on both sides. "P, huh, so does that mean your name starts with a P, like Peter? No, I think Pete suits you better."

Just then William walks up with the key. "Ok, I've got the key". He sees Becky looking at the letter. "We can remove that if you would like."

"Oh, no, I like it, it adds character to the car," Becky says.

"Alright then, let's take…"

"Pete," Becky interjects.

"Pete, for a little drive," William says a bit amused.

Becky gets in behind the wheel and William gets in on the passenger side. The car starts smoothly and Becky eases out into traffic. The car fits her five foot eight frame nicely. It feels good in her hands. They drive around the block as William tells her about the car.

"This is a v6 Dodge Dart, it's five years old and gets excellent gas mileage. It has very low mileage on it for its age. This car will last you a very long time. It's a good midsized car with lots of get-up-and-go." They return from their short trip. "So what do you think? Are you going to take it? You've already named it, I mean, him. You should take him. He really is a good car and he's got a good price. You're not going to find a better price on such a good car anywhere else." William is really spreading it on as he tries to sell her this car.

Becky decides to put William out of his misery and tells him, "Yes, I'll take it."

William says, "Great, let's go write it, . ah.. 'him' up." He leads the way to his sales office. Her credit is good and she is approved for a loan. Then he shows her the payment terms and she signs all the papers. William gives her the keys to her first new used car. She walks out and gets in her car and drives home. She calls Lisa and lets her know she bought a car. Then she goes on line to look for a good rate on car insurance.

On Tuesday, Becky gets a hold of the apartment complex manager and asks about getting a one bedroom apartment. But unfortunately there aren't any available. She is put on a waiting list.

On Wednesday she goes to a second hand store and buys a TV. It's an older model, not too big or too small, nothing fancy, it's not even a flat screen, but it will do. She's not a big TV watcher. The apartment has basic cable included in the rent, which is nice. Otherwise Becky would be limited to what she could get with just an antenna, not that that wouldn't be ok. It's more for the company and noise, so she isn't just rattling around in a quiet apartment.

The rest of the week drags by. Becky settles into her usual routine of get up- go to work- go to the gym- go home- eat- watch some TV- and go to bed. Just to do it all over again the next day.

At last it's Saturday morning. Becky is up and ready to go by 9 am. She is in a nice dress, not too fancy, not to plain. She has washed the overalls and thinks for just a second about wearing them over her dress, but decides that would be embarrassing if anyone else was there at the church, so she puts the folded overalls by the door so she won't forget to take them. It seems weird to go to church so late in the day. She lays down for a minute. Which turns into a couple of hours. When she wakes up, at first she thinks she is late but realizes it is only 11 am. She sits down at her computer and answers her email, does some online shopping, at least "window" shopping. Finally it is time to go and her stomach growls. "Oh, man, I forgot to eat and now it's too late. If I eat something I won't have time to walk to church. Oh, wait, I have Pete my car so I can drive there." She grabs some cereal… "*for lunch?*" She thinks, "*why not ? It's quick and easy.*" She quickly eats, then goes out to her car which doesn't want to start. She thinks, "*Pete, Not now. Oh, God, please let Pete start so I can go worship you,in Jesus' name, amen.*" Just then the car starts. She thanks God and drives the short distance to the home church.

Becky is surprised to see the back yard parking lot so full of cars, but then again it is a back yard and can only hold a few cars. She squeezes into a spot she isn't even sure is suppose to be a parking spot, but it is the only place she can find to park. She is a little nervous about going to this new church, but chastises herself by thinking, "*I've gone to so many new churches, I should be use to this feeling by now*". Still this church is different. She is curious to find out why these people go to church on Saturday instead of Sunday. Becky is greeted at the door by a very friendly older lady named Martha, who instantly takes Becky under her wing and introduces her to "everyone" including Tom. They both play along and try hard not to laugh. She also shows Becky around the house, which Becky already knows, but doesn't want to hurt Martha's feelings, so she "oohs" and "ahs" and says," I see" at all the right places. Becky thanks Martha and finds a place to sit. They sing a lot of songs from a hymnal while Martha plays the piano. People just call out a page number and away they go. Becky even calls out a song. "This is fun and different" Becky thinks. When the people are all sung out, someone says an opening prayer. There is a scripture reading by someone in the congregation and "special request" prayers are asked for and then prayed for. Then one of the other men in the church gives a sermon on "Love and Fear" which Becky finds interesting and different from the other churches she has been to. It contains a lot of scriptures from the Bible which Becky enjoys. They sing more songs and finally close with a prayer. There is a pot luck meal and everyone sits around and talks. Becky counts fifteen people here, of all ages, besides herself.

There are the Wilsons, a family of five, Mom, Julie, and Dad James. They are in their mid to late thirties, Becky guesses. They have three kids; James Jr., better known as J.J. He is12, Samantha is 9, and Charlie 5. The kids are well behaved and not shy around the adults. Charlie takes a shine to Becky and chatters away. Becky thinks he is sweet and laughs at all of his antics.

Then there's the relatively new, newlyweds Patrick (Pat) and Rachel Abbot. Pat is the one who gave the sermon. They are Becky's age. The two women get along very well and Becky feels as if she has found a long lost sister. That is when Charlie lets them get a word in edgewise. Until Julie tells Charlie to leave Ms. Becky alone. Becky politely says, "He's fine." But appreciates the break from the little boy. She enjoys getting to know this new sister she has just meet.

Tom, Becky learns from Rachel, is 28 years old and the son of a preacher.

Martha, the lady that was so nice to Becky when she first came in, Becky learns, is Martha Gracie or "Mom" as everyone calls her. She has a younger sister named Clara Gracie. They are both in their 50s and nether one has ever been married.

There're two other older couples Bob & Libby Bacoda and Blake & Tina Zumiez. They look to be in their mid 40's. Both couples have grown kids that either moved away or are in college or for some other reason don't come to this church.

Last, but certainly not least, is Ms. Marcie Carcie. She is in her 90's. Becky can see that everyone looks after this precious matriarch. Even little Charlie has respect for her. It's not hard to understand why. The lady radiates class and wisdom, like the queen of England.

Becky already feels that she is a part of this unusual group. She feels like she belongs here.

Tom is sitting at the head of the table to the right, then Martha. Becky is next to Martha and Rachel is on the other side of Becky, Pat is on the other end. The tables are narrow, too narrow for anyone to be on the other side and still have room to eat.

Tom relates the story of how he and Becky met, and Martha hits Tom on the shoulder and says, "Tom, you could have told me so I didn't make a fool of myself. Thanks a lot."

Tom rubs his shoulder in mock injury and says, "sorry," as he laughs. Becky thinks he has a marvelous and infectious laugh and he laughs so easily. She really likes that about him, which reminds her of the overalls that she left in the car. She must remember to get them out before she leaves for home.

The food is great and Becky feels a little bad for not bringing some food too, but Martha reassures her that it's fine, "We have plenty of food and you are our guest."

"This meat is so good. What kind is it? I hope it's not pork. I don't eat pork," Becky inquires.

Martha smiles and says, "No, honey, it's not pork. In fact it's not meat at all. We are all vegetarians here. That is imitation meat made out of either tofu which is made out of soy beans, or it's wheat gluten. I'm not sure which, since I didn't bring it, but I'm glad you like it."

"I could easily become a vegetarian with food this good," Becky says, then asks, "So do you eat eggs and cheese? Or are you strict vegans?

"Ms. Marcie is a vegan. That's why she looks so good at 98 years old. The rest of us eat eggs and cheese. In fact Bob and Libby own and run an egg farm. They supply almost all of the grocery stores in town with organic eggs. Anything you want to know about chickens, just ask Bob," Martha says.

Becky says with surprise, "They're Bacoda Farms? That is the only brand of eggs I buy. Wow, that is so cool."

They all laugh and talk for a long time. People seem reluctant to leave, unlike the other churches where everyone is in a hurry to get in and get out and go on their way. Here it's like people check their watches at the door and no one cares what time it is. It is dark outside when people start leaving. Becky finally gets some time to talk to Tom alone as they walk to the two remaining cars in the lot.

"Why do I get the feeling that people have been here since early this morning? What's going on here?" Becky asks.

Tom explains, "The Sabbath begins at sundown on Friday and ends at sundown on Saturday. We love the Sabbath and make the most of it. We start Friday just before sundown with vespers, a way of welcoming in the Sabbath. Which means we sing songs and say prayers as the sun goes down. Then we go home and come back Saturday morning. We share breakfast, have Bible studies, or Sabbath school, as we call it. Sometimes folks go for a walk around the park behind the church, stuff like that. Then everybody comes back to eat a light lunch, have a mini-sermon, and then the main service at 2:00. Then, well you were here for the rest of it. We make a day of it. Luckily we all live close enough so we can do that."

"Wow, this isn't like anything I've heard of before, and you do this every Saturday?" Becky asks.

"Yes, and on the Holy Days too. But I'm way ahead of myself, and its late. I promise if you keep coming we will explain all of it. It's just too much to try to cover right now, or even in one Bible study," Tom replies. "Come by any time tomorrow and I will explain more. Ok?"

"Ok," Becky says as she gets in her car. "I'll see you tomorrow. Will we be doing more yard work as well?" Becky says as she hands Tom the overalls.

"Maybe,.. Probably…I do need to do some," Tom says as he takes the folded overalls. He looks at the bundle Becky has just handed him as if to say, "what's this?" Realizing what it is, he smiles and they both laugh remembering how Becky looked in the oversized clothing. He shuts her door still laughing a little, and walks to his own car. They both leave for their homes.

-4-

In the morning Becky decides not to go to the Sunday church and dresses in blue jeans and a t-shirt. She makes a hardy breakfast for two and packs it in her picnic basket. Then she heads over to the home church.

Tom has just gotten there himself when Becky pulls up. "Hi, you're here early. Nice car, is it new?"

"Thank you, Yes, well it's new to me. I bought him on Monday. His name is Pete thus the P on his side," Becky says.

"Nice, I noticed it yesterday but in the dark I didn't get a good look at it. A Dodge Dart? They're good cars, and I love that you named him. My car has a name too," Tom confesses.

"Really, what is it?" Becky inquires.

"What is what?" Tom teases.

Becky gives Tom an aggravated look and says, "Your car's name, silly."

"Oh, that," Tom says.

"Well,… I'm waiting," Becky says, stifling a smile.

"Ok, I can see you're not the type to let things go. It's .. it's really silly. I haven't told anybody that she has a name."

"It's ok, I don't think it's silly to name things. If it has a personality it deserves a name, no matter what it is. That's my feelings on the matter," Becky encourages.

"Ok, Its Cierra with a C, after my grandmother," Tom says kind of quietly.

"That is a lovely name. I hope your car lives up to her name," Becky states straight faced and serious.

"If you knew my grandmother and my car, you would know it's a perfect fit," Tom says a bit playfully. "Looks like you came to work. What? You didn't want to wear those 'too big' overalls? They're still in my car. I can get them if you want them. They fit you so well and you looked so good in them," Tom teases.

Becky just gives him a look that says, "Really?" and they both laugh.

"Seriously, you look great," Tom says.

Becky turns a bit red and says, "Thank you."

"We can plant some flowers till the others get here," Tom says.

"Others? Who?" Becky asks bewildered.

"I just think it would be best to have someone else here," Tom says, then playfully adds in a funny 'church lady' voice. "What would the neighbors think? The single pastor and a beautiful lady spending hours alone in this house. Scandalous." Then a little more seriously. "Besides, Pat is studying to be a pastor and this will be good practice for him, and Rachel too. You don't mind do you?"

"No, I like Pat and Rachel, it should be fun," Becky says enthusiastically.

"Oh, good, I was a little worried you wouldn't be comfortable with more people here. I'm glad you're fine with it," Tom says as he hulls the plants out to plant in front of the house.

"Wait," Becky says, "If we are going to do all this work, we need, well, I need to start with a good breakfast." Becky brings out her basket.

"Don't think I'm not grateful, but can I ask what's in it?" Tom slyly asks.

"Don't worry, I remember you're all vegetarians, I made egg and cheese burritos, some have mushrooms some don't. I love mushrooms. And a thermos of hot chocolate," Becky tells Tom.

"That sounds yummy, I like mushrooms,.. or not, whichever," Tom says.

They are soon enjoying the egg and cheese burritos, and hot chocolate.

"This is really good, did you make all of this yourself?" Tom asks.

"Thank you, and yes, I did, with my own two hands," Becky brags.

"It's very good, you're going to make some lucky guy a good wife," Tom babbles.

Becky turns red and changes the subject. "This yard is going to look good once the grass seeds start to come up. And with the flowers and other greenery you have here, this place is going to look like a million bucks."

"Thank you," Tom says, "I worked my way through nursing school as a landscaper's helper."

Becky cleans up after their breakfast picnic and puts the basket back in her car. They lay out where to put the different plants then shift them around a few times until they are both happy with how it will look. They go to different ends of the flower bed, start digging holes and putting plants in the holes.

They work toward each other until they meet at the front door. Tom gets out the hose and gives the new plants some water, then they stand back and admire their work. "Looks good," Tom says, "You are a natural at this stuff."

"Thank you," Becky says just as the Abbots drive up.

"Wow, this looks great. You guys got a lot done. Sorry we weren't here to help. We got here as soon as we could," Pat stammers.

"No, you have perfect timing," Tom says.

"I'm all ready to learn things about the Bible," Becky says.

Tom smiles and says, "Shall we go inside or do you all want to sit out here and study."

Rachel says, "It looks great out here, but please let's go inside, I'm afraid my allergies will be driving me crazy in no time if we stay out here."

So they all go in the house church. They sit at one of the long narrow tables in the main room, which doubles as both sanctuary and dining room. Tom is on Becky's left, Rachel is on her right and Pat is on the other side of the narrow table.

Tom, Pat and Rachel all have tablets with Bible apps on them. Becky makes a mental note to bring her tablet with her next time, but first she will have to buy one.

"Wow, Bibles sure have evolved," Becky observes.

Tom says, "I guess so, These make it easier to look things up and jump from translation to translation. But sometimes I like my actual book too. It's easier to make a book your own. Make notes and highlight and stuff."

"I know what you mean," Rachel says, "I just got my tablet, a present from Pat. I'm still learning how to work it."

"So where are you guys?" Pat asks.

Tom says, "Last week we discovered what sin is."

"**1 John 3:4,**" Pat says.

"Right," Tom says, "So now we are about to find out what Jesus said the law is."

"New King James ok with everyone?" Pat asks, as he looks at Becky.

Becky responds, "Sure, that sounds as good as any. How many different translations of the Bible are there? and what's the difference?"

Tom responds, "There are lots of different translations and paraphrases and that's just in English. They all basically say the same thing. Some use more modern up to date terminology. The Old King James uses a lot of words like thee and thou, where we would use 'you', etcetera. The different translations or paraphrases make it easier for people to understand."

Pat interjects, "But some of the paraphrases put their own beliefs into the mix and actually change the original meaning, so it's good to compare the different versions. The Old King James is the best known, but even it has mistranslations. The New King James is the same as the old one, just they changed the language from thee and thou to you. So instead of 'ye shall not' it will say you shall not. For example: **Exodus 22:22 Old King James** reads**, 'Ye shall not afflict any widow, or fatherless child.' New King James** reads, **'you shall not afflict any widows or fatherless child.'** Where the **New Living Translation** reads, **'You must not exploit a widow or an orphan.'** When I have a question on what a verse really means I go to **Young's Literal Translation**. Which reads this same verse as **'Any widow or orphan ye do not afflict.'** But it can get really hard to understand, if that is the only one you read. So the best is to read and compare all of them when there is a question."

"Oh, I see," Becky says, "New King James is fine."

Tom and Rachel both hit their Bible apps on their tablets and place them where Becky can see them too.

"First let's compare what God said in the old testament with what Jesus said in the new," Tom says.

"God said in **Exodus 20:6 (NKJV) 'but showing mercy to thousands, to those who love Me and keep My commandments.**

And Jesus said in **John 14:15 'If you love Me, keep My commandments.**

Hmm, sounds the same to me. What else did Jesus say?

John 14:23&24. 23, Jesus answered and said to him, 'If anyone loves Me, he will keep My word; and My Father will love him, and We will come to him and make Our home with him. 24 He who does not love Me does not keep My words; and the word which you hear is not Mine but the Father's who sent Me.

The Bible tells us that God does not change, so the same God from the old testament is telling Jesus every word to say in the new testament. Like that show on TV 'Repeat After Me'. So the new builds on the old like a house. You don't throw out the strong foundation to build your house on. A house with no foundation would easily get washed away. No, you start with a strong foundation first, then build a house on top of that, and together they make a strong house that withstands the test of time," Tom finishes.

Pat continues with, "**Matthew 22:36 'Teacher, which is the great commandment in the law?' 37. Jesus said to him,**

'You shall love the Lord your God with all your heart, with all your soul, and with all your mind. 38. This is the first and great commandment. 39. And the second is like it: You shall love your neighbor as yourself. 40. On these two commandments hang all the Law and the Prophets.'

Also **Romans 13:10 Love does no harm to a neighbor; therefore love is the fulfillment of the law."**

Tom says, "So how do we show our love to God and to our neighbor?"

Pat answers, **"Matthew 19:16-19 Now behold, one came and said to Him, 'Good Teacher, what good thing shall I do that I may have eternal life?' 17 So He said to him, 'Why do you call Me good? No one is good but One, that is, God. But if you want to enter into life, keep the commandments.' 18 He said to Him, 'Which ones?' Jesus said, 'You shall not murder, You shall not commit adultery, You shall not steal, You shall not bear false witness, 19 Honor your father and your mother, and, You shall love your neighbor as yourself.'"**

Rachel says, "These are part of the ten commandments from the old testament. If these are still in effect then it makes sense that all of the ten are still in effect. For the Bible says in:

Malachi 3:6-7 'For I am the LORD, I do not change; Therefore you are not consumed, O sons of Jacob. 7 Yet from the days of your fathers You have gone away from My ordinances And have not kept them. Return to Me, and I will return to you,' Says the LORD of hosts, and

Hebrews 13:8 Jesus Christ is the same yesterday, today, and forever.

James 2:10 & 11 For whoever shall keep the whole law, and yet stumble in one point, he is guilty of all. 11 For He who said, 'Do not commit adultery,' also said, 'Do not murder.' Now if you do not commit adultery, but you do murder, you have become a transgressor of the law."

"Wait, this all sounds so Jewish," Becky interrupts.

"Yes," Tom states matter-of-factly, "Remember, Jesus was Jewish. We worship a Jewish Messiah. He knew all of the Biblical Laws, His Father wrote those laws. The Bible says when we accept Jesus as our savior, we are grafted into the Israeli 'tree'. In effect we gentiles are adopted Jews.

Romans 11:16-26 NKJV - 16 For if the first fruit is holy, the lump is also holy; and if the root is holy, so are the branches. 17 And if some of the branches were broken off, and you, being a wild olive tree, were grafted in among them, and with them became a partaker of the root and fatness of the olive tree, 18 do not boast against the branches. But if you do boast, remember that you do not support the root, but the root supports you. 19 You will say then, 'Branches were broken off that I might be grafted in.' 20 Well said. Because of unbelief they were broken off, and you stand by faith. Do not be haughty, but fear. 21 For if God did not spare the natural branches, He may not spare you either. 22 Therefore consider the goodness and severity of God: on those who fell, severity; but toward you, goodness, if you continue in His goodness. Otherwise you also will be cut off. 23 And they also, if they do not continue in unbelief, will be grafted in, for God is able to graft them in again. 24 For if you were cut out of the olive tree which is wild by nature, and were

grafted contrary to nature into a cultivated olive tree, how much more will these, who are natural branches, be grafted into their own olive tree? 25 For I do not desire, brethren, that you should be ignorant of this mystery, lest you should be wise in your own opinion, that blindness in part has happened to Israel until the fullness of the Gentiles has come in. 26 And so all Israel will be saved, as it is written: 'The Deliverer will come out of Zion, And He will turn away ungodliness from Jacob;'

We just read that '**Jesus is the same yesterday, today and forever.'**

If being Jewish was good enough for my savior, Then I am honored to be considered Jewish as well," Tom finishes.

"Oh," Becky says reflectively. "The churches I went to always made it sound like being Jewish was bad. That it was the Jews that killed Jesus. A lot of Christians seem almost prejudiced against Jews."

"If you're against Jews, you're against Jesus. Like it or not Jesus was a Jew. He was a Jews' Jew. He was the perfect Jew. Which means he not only kept all of the Biblical laws, he kept them perfectly. We can only try to lamely follow. As far as who killed Him, I'm afraid anyone who has ever sinned is guilty of nailing him to the cross, for he died for all of us sinners. No, the Jews didn't kill Jesus, I killed Jesus," Pat declares.

"Wow!" Becky says with her eyes wide open." I never heard that or thought of that. When you put it like that, I guess it's a good thing to learn about old testament ways and laws. Especially if you want to know more about Jesus, who he was and what he stood for."

"Exactly, so, what else does the new testament say about the old testament Laws?" Tom asks. then reads,

"Matthew 5:17-19, 21-22, 27-28, 33-39, 43-44, 46-48, - 17 Do not think that I came to destroy the Law or the Prophets. I did not come to destroy but to fulfill. So what does it mean to fulfill the law? Lets read on and see what Jesus says. **18 For assuredly, I say to you, till heaven and earth pass away, one jot or one title will by no means pass from the law till all is fulfilled.** The law is the same yesterday, today, and until the end of this age when Jesus comes back and establishes his kingdom on this earth.' Lets read on. **19 Whoever therefore breaks one of the least of these commandments, and teaches men, so shall be called least in the kingdom of God; but whoever does and teaches them, he shall be called great in the kingdom of God. ... 21 You have heard that it was said to those of old, You shall not murder, and whoever murders will be in danger of the judgment. 22 But I say to you that whoever is angry with his brother without a cause shall be in danger of the judgment. And whoever says to his brother, 'Raca!' shall be in danger of the council. But whoever says, 'You fool!' shall be in danger of the lake of fire. ...**

The New Living Translation, or NLT, puts it this way **'But I say, if you are even angry with someone, you are subject to judgment! If you call someone an idiot, you are in danger of being brought before the court, and if you curse someone, you are in danger of the lake of fire.'**

And Young's Literal Translation, or YLT, reads, **'But I say to you, that everyone who is angry at his brother without cause,** That's important, **shall be in danger of the judgment,**

and whoever may say to his brother, Empty fellow! Shall be in danger of the Sanhedrim, and whoever may say, Rebel! shall be in danger of the Gehenna of the fire.' We'll cover the Gehenna fire later. It's ok to get mad or angry, if you have a valid reason or a good cause. It's what you do with that anger that matters. We are to get mad and still not sin. Jesus got mad. But not when he was personally attacked, no, he got mad when people treated his father without respect. But that's a whole different subject. Getting back to the **New King James**?

27. (NKJV) 'You have heard that it was said to those of old, You shall not commit adultery.' 28 But I say to you that whoever looks at a woman to lust for her has already committed adultery with her in his heart. ... 33 Again you have heard that it was said to those of old, 'You shall not swear falsely, but shall perform your oaths to the Lord.' 34 But I say to you, do not swear at all: neither by heaven, for it is God's throne; 35 nor by the earth, for it is His footstool; nor by Jerusalem, for it is the city of the great King. 36 Nor shall you swear by your head, because you cannot make one hair white or black. 37 But let your 'Yes' be 'Yes,' and your 'No, No.' For whatever is more than these is from the evil one. 38 You have heard that it was said, 'An eye for an eye and a tooth for a tooth.' 39 But I tell you not to resist an evil person. But whoever slaps you on your right cheek, turn the other to him also. ... 43 You have heard that it was said, 'You shall love your neighbor and hate your enemy.' 44 But I say to you, love your enemies, bless those who curse you, do good to those who hate you, and pray for those who spitefully use you

and persecute you, '... 46 For if you love those who love you, what reward have you? Do not even the tax collectors do the same? 47 And if you greet your brethren only, what do you do more than others? Do not even the tax collectors do so? 48 Therefore you shall be perfect, just as your Father in heaven is perfect.

We cannot reach perfection in this life time. We can only strive toward it, not to be saved, but because we are saved and want to please our Father in Heaven. Because God wants us to have the best life and be the best person we can be. The old testament gave us the letter of the law. Jesus gave us the spirit of the law. I think what Jesus meant by 'fulfill' the law according to the rest of the chapter was, and is, to make them fuller. At the end of the age, When Jesus returns, then all of the laws will be accomplished. Does this make sense to everyone?" Tom asks.

Rachel interjects, "I think since Jesus was the only one to ever live a perfect sinless life, that he is the only one to fulfill or 'live' all of Gods laws flawlessly."

"That is very good insight, Rachel. I never thought of it that way, but it makes perfect sense to me. Thank you. Are we ready to read through the 'ten' and read what the letter of the law says, then see if we can figure out what the spirit of the law might be?" Tom finishes. Everyone nods.

Pat reads, "1st commandment. **Exodus 20:1-3 And God spoke all these words, saying:"**

"Wait, who spoke them? God! not Moses? So these are Gods laws, not Moses' law, as some churches want to say they are," Tom interjects, "Please continue".

Pat reads, **"2, I am the LORD your God, who brought you out of the land of Egypt, out of the house of bondage. 3 You shall have no other gods before Me.**

1 Corinthians 8:5 NKJV - 5 For even if there are so-called gods, whether in heaven or on earth (as there are many gods and many lords),"

Tom asks, "What other gods could come between you and God? Or should I say gods we might put before or in front of God?"

Becky answers, half questioning. "Satan?"

Tom says, "Yes, he is the ultimate one to come between us and God. Though most people don't realize they are letting Satan come between them and God, but when we let other things come between us and God it is actually Satan and his plan at work to destroy our relationship with God. Who or what else can we put before God?"

Becky, "His demons?"

"Yes, demons often come to people as gods and want to be worshiped. Where do you think all those pagan gods from mythology came from? Who else?" Tom asks.

Becky says, "I don't know."

"Pat, what do you think?" Tom asks.

"Angels," Pat answers.

"Yes," Tom says, "Who else?"

Rachel says, "Wait, how can angels come between us and God?"

"Good question," Tom says. "Pat, can you answer that?"

"I know angels don't intend to come between us and God, but if one is suddenly face to face with an angel, especially now when we don't see angels as angels, he or she is probably going to think this magnificent being is a god. It would be easy for one to worship that being as a god. Even though that is not the intention of the angel," Pat explains. "Even the apostles tried to worship angels when they saw them. Let's look at:

Revelation 19:10 NKJV - 10 And I fell at his feet to worship him. But he said to me, 'See that you do not do that! I am your fellow servant, and of your brethren who have the testimony of Jesus. Worship God! For the testimony of Jesus is the spirit of prophecy.'

Revelation 22:8 Now I, John, saw and heard these things. And when I heard and saw, I fell down to worship before the feet of the angel who showed me these things. 9 Then he said to me, 'See that you do not do that. For I am your fellow servant, and of your brethren the prophets, and of those who keep the words of this book. Worship God.'"

Rachel says, "Oh,.. well, when you put it that way, I can see how angels could be worshiped as gods, and therefore put before God."

Becky asks, "What about other saints, like Jesus' mother Mary?"

"Yes, but remember those people are dead. They cannot be gods, though people do worship them. They also worship death. But that is for the next commandment," Tom says.

Pat says, "The one most mainstream churches worship is Jesus."

"Jesus? But Jesus and God are the same aren't they?" Becky asks bewildered.

Pat says, "The Bible says that the father and the son are two different beings. There is only one God the Father. And

No man comes to the Father except through the Son. If they are the same being then that wouldn't make any sense. And who did Jesus pray to when he prayed, which he did all the time, if they are the same person?

John 4:34 NKJV - 34 Jesus said to them, 'My food is to do the will of Him who sent Me, and to finish His work.'"

"Jesus mentions God as 'My Father' over thirty times in the new testament," Tom says, then reads.

"Luke 10:22 All things have been delivered to Me by My Father, and no one knows who the Son is except the Father, and who the Father is except the Son, and the one to whom the Son wills to reveal Him.

John 20:17 Jesus said to her, "Do not cling to Me, for I have not yet ascended to My Father; but go to My brethren and say to them, 'I am ascending to My Father and your Father, and to My God and your God.'

Hebrews 1:3 who being the brightness of His glory and the express image of His person, and upholding all things by the word of His power, when He had by Himself purged our sins, sat down at the right hand of the Majesty on high,

Revelation 22:3 NKJV - 3 And there shall be no more curse, but the throne of God <u>and of the Lamb</u> shall be in it, and His servants shall serve Him."

Tom continues, "If God and Jesus are the same, how can he sit at God's right hand? Let me put it this way. You came from your mother, so does that mean you and your mother are the same person? You may look alike, you may sound alike, and you may even be like minded, but you are not the same person, no matter how close you are to each other. The same thing goes for Jesus."

Becky, looking a little bewildered, asks Rachel, "Can I borrow your tablet for just a second?"

Rachel says, "Sure," and hands Becky her tablet.

Becky types in some words in the search box, hits enter, scrolls down and with an "Aha," says, "but it says right here in **John 10:30 NKJV - 30 'I and My Father are one.'** How do you explain that?" as she hands the tablet back to Rachel.

Pat says, "The Bible says in **Genesis 2:24 NKJV - 24 Therefore a man shall leave his father and mother and be joined to his wife, and they shall become one flesh.** Does that mean they literally become one person?"

Becky answers, "No, that's a metaphor it means they become like minded, or they come together and the two make a baby, that is one made from the two of them. Oh, I don't know how to explain it. I've never been married."

"I understand what you are saying," Pat says, "I think its along the same lines that Jesus said **'I and my Father are one'** they are so close that they know each other's thoughts and they mirror each other in looks, if God has a look. The Bible says God is invisible, at least to us he is. The Bible says in **John 6:46 NKJV - 'Not that anyone has seen the Father, except He who is from God; He has seen the Father.'** But just as God's spirit lives in us, Jesus had Gods spirit living in him to the fullest degree. I think it's like in **Genesis 2:24.** It's not literally that they are one person, it's "like" they are one person. Jesus came from God. He is his only begotten son and the only man to have seen God. Who or what Jesus was before he was born of Mary is unclear. The Bible says Jesus "was" from the beginning, as God the Father has no beginning and no end. So it appears that Jesus also has no beginning and no end. **Revelation 22:13 NKJV - 13 'I am the Alpha and the Omega, the Beginning and the End, the First and the Last.'** Was he always God's son or did he become God's son at his birth as a mortal being? I don't know. The Bible isn't clear as to who or what Jesus was before. They could have been one being before his birth but **John 1:2 NKJV - 2 He was in the beginning with God.** Makes it sound like they were two separate beings. That's something we can ask him when we see him. Am I making sense?" Pat asks.

"I guess that makes sense," Becky says, "I just never heard that before."

Pat continues, "That doesn't diminish what Jesus did for us. In fact it enhances what he did. Just think, the greatest being ever, with only one being greater and that's God himself, gave up everything to humble himself and become a mere mortal to be tortured and die a criminal's death for us because he loves us and wants us to be with him and our Father forever. We are to be forever grateful and thank Jesus daily for giving us a way to our Father. Without him we would be forever separated from our Father because of sin. We just can't stop there and only worship Jesus, we are to cross the bridge on the Cross that bridges the great divide and go on to our Father who made us and not have any other gods before or above or greater then God the Father, including Jesus. Yes, I love my big brother, I just love God my true father more."

Tom says," As I see it, there are basically four approaches man takes to God.

1. It is to ignore God and live our life as we see fit, usually doing our own thing without regard for God or His Laws or anyone else.
2. It is to try to earn our way to what we perceive as heaven, but this can never get us there. There is no way we can "be good" our way to God.

Isaiah 64:6 NKJV - 6 But we are all like an unclean thing, And all our righteousnesses are like filthy rags; We all fade as a leaf, And our iniquities, like the wind, Have taken us away.

In the beginning God and man walked together for man was good. Then man sinned and a great rift happened between us and God that cannot be bridged by anything mere man can do. It took a supernatural act from God by sending his Son to bridge the gap with his own life. That is why no man can come to the Father except through the Son.

3. The third thing people do is come to Jesus, but they stop there and just worship Jesus without going any further. But Jesus said in **Matthew 19:17 Why do you call me Good? No one is good but One, that is God.** And **Matthew 4:10 NKJV - 10 Then Jesus said to him, "Away with you, Satan! For it is written, 'You shall worship the LORD your God, and Him only you shall serve.'** Jesus didn't say you are to worship me and me only. No, he said, worship the Father God and Him only. We are to worship God the Father and have no other gods before him, and that includes Jesus.

4. I believe in the fourth approach. We are to come to Jesus to be cleansed of our sins by his blood, then after he has made us white as snow, we are to go across the bridge that

Jesus provides and go to our Heavenly Father directly and worship only him.

Does that make sense?" Tom asks.

"Yes,.. yes that does," Becky says.

"Good, now for the next commandment. Rachel, will you do the honors?" Tom asks.

Rachel reads, " #2. **Exodus 20:4-6 'You shall not make for yourself a carved image-of-any likeness of anything that is in heaven above, or that is in the earth beneath, or that is in the water under the earth; 5. you shall not bow down to them nor serve them. For I, the LORD your God, am a jealous God, visiting the iniquity of the fathers upon the children to the third and fourth generations of those who hate Me, 6. but showing mercy to thousands, to those who love Me and keep My commandments."**

"The letter of the law states we are not to bow down to statues that we have made or had made for us by a skilled artist. Which in this day and age most people don't do. But we certainly make gods out of other things. What do you think we can make as a god that can come between us and God in this day?" Tom asks the group.

Pat says, "This is where the worship of Jesus' Mother Mary and the other saints comes in."

"Yes, this is true. What else?" Tom asks.

"Or even 'so-called or self-proclaimed' living prophets of today," Rachel adds.

Becky says with more confidence, "I know about that one. There are some really out-there religions today."

"Yes, that there are," Pat agrees. "But we must remember that in all Christian religions and denominations there is some good, some truth, and things we can learn. Example: we got our Bible as we know it today from the Catholics. And the Mormons are some of the most loving people you can know. Jesus said in

John 13:34-35 NKJV - 34 'A new commandment I give to you, that you love one another; as I have loved you, that you also love one another. 35 By this all will know that you are My disciples, if you have love for one another.'

And the Baptists preserved water immersion baptism. Without them we would all be splattered with water instead of immersed," Pat finishes.

"We are told not to judge, but to love, to find 'the positive' in everything," Tom says.

"We are also told to 'work out our own salvation' **Philippians 2:12 NKJV - 12 Therefore, my beloved, as you have always obeyed, not as in my presence only, but now much more in my absence, work out your own salvation with fear and trembling;** which I think means we are to learn what 'God wants from us and then do it, as Abraham did, God didn't ask everyone to do what Abraham did, He just asked Abraham, and he did it without question." Rachel says.

"Exactly, what else can we put before God?" Pat asks.

"How about TV, people will stay home and watch 'whatever' on TV rather than go to church," Becky states.

"Good one," Tom says, "what else?"

"There's all kinds of things that can come between us and God. We even call singers 'idols' these days, movie stars, sports stars, boyfriends, girlfriends. Even a car or some other possession, just about anything or anybody can come between us and God," Rachel says.

Pat says, "I think the biggest idol or obstacle that stands between me and God is… myself. Sometimes I would rather do what I want to do than do what God wants me to do. I make a god of Myself."

"This is so true. That is something we all have to work on overcoming daily. I think you are right about that one," Tom says. "What do you think Becky"

"Wow, that is so true. I know that is my greatest obstacle. Something I defiantly hadn't thought of until now," Becky says.

"Are we ready for number three?" Rachel asks.

"Sure," Tom says. "I'll read the next one, if that's ok?"

Everyone indicates that's fine and Tom reads.

"Number 3, **Exodus 20: 7 You shall not take the name of the LORD your God in vain, for the LORD will not hold him guiltless who takes His name in vain.**

"Obviously, the letter of the law people think means don't swear or curse." Tom continues, "but what do you think the spirit of the law means?"

Rachel says after a time of silence. "I think it means don't call yourself a Christian or child of God just to get something, or gain notoriety, or whatever. If you don't really mean it, don't say you are God's when all you want is to trick people into sending you money, or get people to trust you just so you can get something from them."

"What do you think Becky?" Tom asks.

"That makes sense, but I still think it's wrong to swear using God or Jesus' name," Becky says.

"Of course, but I think it is both," Rachel says.

"Me too," Pat and Tom add. Becky nods in agreement.

Pat reads number 4. **"Exodus 20:8-11 Remember the Sabbath day, to keep it holy. 9. Six days you shall labor and do all your work, 10. but the seventh day is the Sabbath of the LORD your God. In it you shall do no work: you, nor your son, nor your daughter, nor your male servant, nor your female servant, nor your cattle, nor your stranger who is within your gates. 11. For in six days the LORD made the heavens and the earth, the sea, and all that is in them, and rested the seventh day. Therefore the LORD blessed the Sabbath day and hallowed it."**

Becky reads and re-reads this one. Then she looks at the calendar on the wall and sees that the seventh day of the week isn't Sunday, no, it's actually the first day of the week. The seventh day is Saturday. She has never read this or heard this from anyone before.

"I can see you have a lot of questions about this one, that is why I think we should discuss this one after we cover all the others," Tom says.

Becky sighs, "Ok, I guess. But I really want to know more about this."

"I promise we will cover the Sabbath in full next time," Tom says.

"These first four are how we show our love for God." Tom relays. "The next six are how we show our love for our neighbor. Who wants to read Exodus 20:12?"

"I will," Becky offers. Tom nods his approval and Becky reads.

"#5. **Exodus 20:12 Honor your father and your mother, that your days may be long upon the land which the LORD your God is giving you.**

This one seems pretty straight forward to me. We are to honor our parents in all that we do. We may still go our own way, but we aren't too 'bad mouth' or put our parents down to others in any way. Right?" Becky finishes.

Rachel asks, "But what if your parents are not honorable people? What if they steal things and teach you to steal, or they kill people and try to get you to kill too. Or what if they are abusive and hurt you, making you hate them?"

Becky turns and looks intently at Tom for an answer to this one.

Tom says, "The Bible says in **Ephesians 6:4 And you, fathers, do not provoke your children to wrath, but bring them up in the training and admonition of the Lord.** And,

Colossians 3:21 Fathers, do not provoke your children, lest they become discouraged.

The Bible also says in **Romans 12:19 Beloved, do not avenge yourselves, but rather give place to wrath; for it is written, 'Vengeance is Mine, I will repay,' says the Lord.**

Hebrews 10:30 For we know Him who said, 'Vengeance is Mine, I will repay,' says the Lord. And again, 'The LORD will judge His people.'

The word 'Forgive' is in the Bible 53 times in 45 verses. The ones that apply here are: **Matthew 6:12, 14 & 15. 12 And forgive us our debts, (or sins) As we forgive our debtors . ... 14 For if you forgive men their trespasses (sins), your heavenly Father will also forgive you. 15 But if**

you do not forgive men their trespasses, neither will your Father forgive your trespasses.

If our parents do wrong it is in God's hands to deal with them, not ours. We are told, commanded even, to forgive them, even if they don't ask for forgiveness. Even though they sinned, we can only control ourselves not others, so we are, even under these circumstances, told 'not to sin'. The old adage says, 'if you can't say something nice, don't say anything at all.' That applies here. Saying things like 'they did the best that they could.' When confronted is one way of honoring them. But that is a good question and a hard one to answer. I think under that situation each person has to work out their own salvation. As it says in **Philippians 2:12 '** I'm afraid this is a simplified answer to a very complex question. If someone is facing that problem they should seek counseling and work out their own solution." Tom finishes.

Every one gives a thoughtful nod.

Then Pat reads; "#6**. Exodus 20:13 You shall not murder**. This is different from don't kill. Killing and murder or not quite the same. True both end in death but it's the motive and reason behind the death that is at stake here. You can kill a mosquito, or a fly because it bit you, or a cow so you can eat it. If you murder someone, you think about it and plan it out in hate. Jesus talked about this one as we read earlier, he said**, 'If you even hate someone in your heart you are guilty of murder**.' That's what this is saying to me anyway. The Bible does give people an out for accidental death that you may have a hand in, or self defense. These are not considered murder. Murder is premeditated," Pat concludes.

"So the moral of this one is don't hate anyone," Tom says. " In fact we are commanded to love every one . Love does no harm. Murder is defiantly doing harm."

Rachel asks, "What about abortion?"

Tom states, "Abortion is murder. Abortion happens because a child is conceived and then someone decides the child is an inconvenience. It is very easy to kill an extremely helpless child that is still in the womb. You can't get rid of one sin by committing another sin. There are other ways of dealing with an unwanted child. Every child deserves to be wanted, at the same time every life is precious and deserves a chance at life."

Becky asks, "What about rape? What if a pregnancy happens because a woman was raped"

Tom again replies, "Rape is wrong. Rape is a sin. But if you were sitting in a restaurant and a burglar walks in and demands all of your money and leaves, you're not going to turn to your son and say 'it's all your fault you wanted to come here' and then pull out a gun and shoot him. The son is innocent. He had no way of knowing you were going to be robbed, so why would you punish him with death? It's the same for an innocent child in the womb. Why would you murder a totally innocent child for something he or she had no control over? Find the man that did the crime and punish him. Make him pay child support and I think he should be castrated as well, but that's my opinion. If a child is not wanted for any reason, put him or her up for adoption. Don't commit murder."

Rachel asks, "Is there any reason for abortion?"

Pat chimes in with, "I would guess if having the child is absolutely going to cause the mother to die, then it might be justified. But I think everything medically possible should be done to save both the mother and the child. Only as a last resort should abortion be done."

"I wish science would invent an artificial womb to put these babies in so everyone could get what they want," Tom says sadly.

Becky quietly asks, "What about miscarriages?"

Pat answers, "A miscarriage is no one's fault. I guess you could say it was an act of God. I think it is an act of nature. Who knows why a woman would miscarry? But I'm sure there is no sin in that, unless the mother or someone else does something to purposely make the child abort. Then it is no longer a miscarriage but an abortion."

Rachel asks, "What if the child is going to be severely handicapped?'

Pat says, "I don't think even that is a reason to kill it. There are things people can do. The child still deserves the best life it can have. No matter what, God still loves them just as much. Next to God we are all severely handicapped."

Rachel thinks about it for a minute, and says, "When you put it that way, I guess you are right."

Tom quietly asks, "Are we ready to go on to the next one?"

"Ok," Rachel says and reads, "# 7**. Exodus 20:14. You shall not commit adultery."**

"Question," Becky asks, "If you are single and your boyfriend is single and you have sex, is that adultery?"

Tom says, "Jesus said in **Matthew 5:28 But I say, anyone who even looks at a woman with lust has already**

committed adultery with her in his heart." There is no stipulation as to the marital status of the man or the woman in this statement."

Rachel says, "So the Bible says if you look at a person with lust in your heart you have committed adultery. And in other places the Bible talks about other sexual sins, and what to do and what not to do. The Bible also says in other places that we are to stay pure, that sex is to be a beautiful thing between a husband and a wife only. Let me read,

"Genesis 2:23-24 And Adam said: 'This is now bone of my bones And flesh of my flesh; She shall be called Woman, Because she was taken out of Man.' 24 Therefore a man shall leave his father and mother and be joined to his wife, and they shall become one flesh."

Tom says, "Thank you, Rachel. If you want to know more on what God says is an abomination read **Leviticus 20.** Basically sex outside of marriage is wrong. Be it with another person, or a thing, or even an animal. We have more of the ten to cover."

"Ok," the group says.

Becky reads, "# 8. **Exodus 20:15. "You shall not steal."**

"Again love does no harm. Stealing something from someone that worked hard for it is doing harm. I'm sure the same attitude toward adultery applies here. If you look at something that does not belong to you with coveting in your heart, you have already stolen it as far as God is concerned," Tom explains, "Are we clear on this one, or do we want to discuss it?"

Becky says, "I have one question about this. If I'm out of work and I'm homeless and starving, is it ok to steal something to eat, or am I expected to starve to death?"

Rachel says, "In all cases, we are to trust in God for all of our needs, He knows what we need, we just need more faith. In the old days there were laws to provide for the poor, like **Leviticus 19:9 NKJV - 9 'When you reap the harvest of your land, you shall not wholly reap the corners of your field, nor shall you gather the gleanings of your harvest.'** The bible says it is to be left for the poor. Today we have several organizations that deal with just that problem. There are too many places to go to get a free meal, it would be hard to justify theft in that instance. Ask and it shall be given unto you. So, no, we really can't justify stealing under any circumstance."

"But also remember that God looks at our heart and our motives for doing anything and everything we do. He is our ultimate judge and the one to whom we will eventually have to answer," Tom says, " but, yes, theft is wrong."

"People can come up with all kinds of things to self justify their actions. But when you look at it through the light of Gods eyes, wrong is just wrong," Pat states.

Pat continues, "# 9**. Exodus 20:16. You shall not bear false witness against your neighbor."**

"I think this means you should not lie. Sometimes you can lie by not saying anything, if you know that you did it, or who did, especially in court. But if you are not in court and there is no crime to report on, and telling the truth is going to hurt someone, isn't it better to say something nice or not say anything at all than to hurt them needlessly?" Becky states.

"Yes, we are to weigh everything we do or say with love. Needlessly hurting someone's feelings for the sake of 'truth' isn't love. You may be acting out of meanness, or even hate. But if you are in a court of law, you must tell the truth," Pat says.

"Or in business," Rachel chimes in. "We are told to treat everyone fairly and not to cheat people, by putting our thumb on the scale when weighing out grain, etcetera. **Leviticus 19:13 NKJV - 13 'You shall not cheat your neighbor, nor rob him. The wages of him who is hired shall not remain with you all night until morning.**"

"Yes, lying and cheating are wrong, but we are to be gentle when it comes to someone's feelings, and sometimes people will set us up to either be hurt or to hurt someone else. Human nature is a fickle thing. Some people will say the wrong thing no matter what they say, while other people can say anything and it comes out in such a way that no one is offended" Tom says. "But in the long run truth is always best if doled out in love."

"That's a lot to think about." Becky says. "I think this is the hardest commandment to live up to in our day to day lives."

"I think the next one is the hardest," Pat confesses. "It reads…

"10. Exodus 20:17 You shall not covet your neighbor's house; you shall not covet your neighbor's wife, nor his male servant, nor his female servant, nor his ox, nor his donkey, nor anything that is your neighbor's.

"If you walk by the home of someone that has more than you do, it's hard not to wish that was yours. But we don't know what they did to get there. Did they steal it? Or cheat their way into getting it? In which case we should feel sorry for them. Or did they work hard in an honest way to achieve their wealth? In that case we should feel happy for them, not envious. We should learn from them, not try to tear them down, or steal from them. In either case we are told not to covet what they have, no matter how they got it. Coveting comes first in all of these crimes against our neighbors. First we covet, then we become obsessed with having it, then we take it. That's how the world is. But God's church is different. If we let Gods spirit control us, we will not sin," Pat says.

Tom asks, "Becky, after all of this do you think the ten commandments are relative for today, or not?"

Becky says without hesitation, "Of course they are. It was wrong to steal then and it is still wrong to steal today, or murder, or have gods before The Father God. So yes, the ten are still relevant for today. I'm just not sure what the fourth one is all about."

Rachel says, "Well, we certainly have a lot to think about, but I'm really getting hungry. Can we stop here and go get something to eat?"

Tom and Pat both say, "That sounds good to me."

Becky says, "But what about the Sabbath? I want to know more." At that moment her stomach growls loudly. "Well, I guess I'm hungry too."

Everyone laughs, Pat suggests, "Why don't we all go out to eat? I know this nice Mexican restaurant not far from here. We can all go in my car."

"Ok," Tom and Rachel say enthusiastically.

Becky starts trying to think of an excuse not to go. She is on a strict budget and eating out isn't in the budget. Then as if reading her mind Rachel says, "Becky, you have to come with us. I really want to get to know you better. It will be fun."

Becky relents, "Ok, you win." As she thinks, "*I'll just get some chips and salsa.*"

Pat says "Good, I get to show off my new car."

Tom and Pat walk out together. "You have a new car? What did you get? When did you get it?" Tom asks.

Pat laughs as they go out and can't be heard any more.

Rachel and Becky pick up the tablets that the men left behind. Rachel says, "I'm so glad you are coming too. I think being with those two would drive me crazy with all the car talk. Honestly they are like two kids with a new toy." The women laugh, Becky says, "I have to admit I'm curious about the new car too." The women go out and Rachel locks the door behind her. They all pile into Pat and Rachel's new white SUV. The men in front and the women in the back. Tom and Pat are chattering away about the new car, gas mileage, etc. The car is luxurious.

Pat says, "It's a Range Rover, it has four wheel drive for going off road. It's a V6 so it has lots of power, built in GPS, rear back up camera, park assist, all the bells and whistles. Top safety rating too."

Tom says, "It's very roomy. A guy can really stretch out in here," as he stretches his legs.

As the guys talk about cars, Rachel engages Becky in conversation about her life.

"So Becky, tell me about yourself?"

"There's not much to tell. I was born here. I'm an only child. I accepted Christ a couple months ago and have been looking for a church home since," Becky says, "I want to know about you. How did you and Pat meet?"

"We are high school sweet hearts. We went to the same college. And we've been married for one year as of tomorrow," Rachel says.

"Wow, congratulations, happy anniversary," Becky says.

"Thank you," Rachel says.

"We are here," Pat announces from the front seat. He parks the Rover and they all go into the family style Mexican Restaurant, called "El Casa Valdez".

Pat goes to the front desk and says, "The Abbot party"

The man behind the desk says "Yes sir, right this way" He leads the group to a private room where Pat and Rachel's family's are already gathered.

"Surprise," Pat and Rachel quietly say to Tom and Becky.

Tom and Becky don't know what to say, and stand there speechless.

Rachel's dad, Mr. Valdez, the owner of the restaurant, says, "Come in sit down. Now that the couple of honor is here, let's all eat." The family and friends of Pat and Rachel that are gathered there get up and head to the two buffet tables. Mr. Valdez explains one table is the meat table for the meat eaters and the other table is all vegetarian. "Thanks to my daughter and son-in-law this restaurant is now vegetarian friendly."

Becky and Tom look at Pat and Rachel who smile and say, "Sorry we tricked you but we didn't think you would come if we told you the truth," Pat says.

Rachel adds, "And we really wanted you guys to come. You are our friends too and our church family. We couldn't think of having an anniversary party without you."

Everyone gets their food and sit back down and start eating the very good food. Becky hasn't seen so many different vegetarian Mexican dishes before in her life. She takes a little of everything. Pat and Rachel are ushered to the front of the table. Tom and Becky find two seats near the back of the second table. Everyone is dressed in their fine clothes. Even Rachel and Pat look nice, while Tom and Becky are in their grubby work-in-the-yard clothes, which makes Becky a little self conscious, ok, a lot self conscious, but everyone else ignores what they are wearing and treats them like family. Soon Becky and Tom are relaxed and enjoy the food and the company. Mr. Valdez stands and calls for silence. "Friends and family, we are here to celebrate Rachel and Patrick's first anniversary. Even though I was skeptical of this guy at first he has proven to be a good husband, provider, and son-in-law. Rachel you did good."

Mr. Abbot stands and says, "We fell in love with Rachel from the beginning. We are so pleased to call her our daughter. She is sweet and kind and the perfect wife for our oldest boy. And knowing the Valdez family has been a great pleasure too, for both our spirits and our waistlines." As he pulls at his tight belt. Everyone laughs, and he sits back down. The mariachi band files in and starts to play as different ones get up to dance. The festivities go on for some time until the desserts are brought out. As people are deciding what to get, Pat stands and taps his glass with his knife and says, "Attention, please. First, I want to say, this party is great, thank you. Really, I am so blessed having Rachel as my wife. Life is perfect, I have a beautiful wife, a job I love, especially now with the new promotion, which gives us enough money so Rachel can quit her job here, and stay home, and raise our baby that will be here in about seven months."

At that point both Mrs. Valdez and Mrs. Abbot stand up and say, "We're going to be grandparents!" Then they both scream and hug each other, then they hug Rachel and Pat and jump up and down all at the same time.

Pat jokingly says, "Sorry you're so disappointed." At that the women scream in delight again and hug the couple again. Then the two women go huddle off in a corner to start planning for their grandchild, which gives everyone else a chance to congratulate the couple. The festivities would have continued all night, but Pat says, "I'm sorry to have to be the wet blanket here, but some of us have jobs we have to go to in the morning, and our new mom-to-be needs her beauty sleep. She is sleeping for two now." People giggle. Then more quietly Pat asks Tom and Becky, "Are you guys ready to go?"

"Yes," they both say, and the four head out to Pat and Rachel's car. Once inside the quiet car Tom says, "Now I know how you can afford this fancy new toy. A big promotion, hmm?"

"Yep," Pat says. The two men talk on while the girls talk in the back.

Becky takes Rachel's hands and says, "You're pregnant? That's fantastic, I'm so excited for you. What are you hoping for? How many kids do you want?" Becky babbles.

Rachel laughs and says, "Yes, I'm really pregnant. I don't care if it's a boy or a girl, as long as it's healthy. Pat and I both come from big families so we both want a big family. I really don't have a number in mind, I guess we will take it one baby at a time." They both giggle and Becky hugs Rachel.

"You know I'm here for you. Anything I can do just let me know. Ok?" Becky tells Rachel.

"Thanks, Bek," Rachel says as she starts tearing up "That means a lot, you're such a good friend." Then regaining her composure and blowing her nose, she continues, "Sorry, my hormones are all messed up. I cry at everything."

"Wow, you really are pregnant," Becky says, and Rachel laughs more then she should.

They reach the church, and Tom and Becky get out of the car and head to their cars. Becky tells Tom, "I didn't know Rachel was Mexican? But I'm terrible when it comes to telling ethnic people apart. People are just people to me."

"I think that's the way it should be," Tom says, "I didn't know her parents owned El Casa Valdez? That's like the best Mexican Restaurant in town, in the whole region as a matter of fact. Both families are very well off. We were hobnobbing with the elite tonight, my dear girl."

"And yet they are all so down to earth," Becky adds.

"Yes, they are. That's an unexpected pleasant surprise," Tom says, "Well, here we are at our cars. So I guess I'll see you next Sabbath?"

"That's so far away," Becky says "Would it be possible to meet before then? I'm very anxious to hear more about the Sabbath."

"Ok, when is good for you?" Tom asks.

"Any day is good for me. I don't have any commitments after work. At least nothing I can't work around," Becky says.

"Ok, how about tomorrow at your place, at 7pm," Tom suggests.

"Make it 6 and I will cook supper for you," Becky says.

"Sounds good. Mind if I bring Martha along?" Tom asks.

"No, not at all. I had a great time with Pat and Rachel. I learned a lot. I know I can learn a lot from Ms. Martha too," Becky says, "Martha is a very sweet lady."

"See you then," Tom says.

"Wait," Becky shouts, as Tom starts to go to his car.

Tom turns back around and says, "What?"

"Here, this is my address and apt. number, and cell phone number too." Becky hands Tom her card.

"Oh, yes, that would be helpful. Thanks," Tom says as he takes the card. They both leave.

-5-

Work on Monday is a blur to Becky. She kind-of remembers telling Lisa about the Bible study and the next thing she knows Lisa is coming too. Becky doesn't think it will be a problem. So she doesn't think to tell Tom, Lisa is coming.

After work Becky does a quick stop at the store, then high-tails it home to start cooking spaghetti for four.

Lisa shows up first, and immediately starts helping Becky get things ready.

"Lisa, you are such a good friend, I don't know why I'm so nervous," Becky states.

"That's ok, that's what friends are for," Lisa says and smiles.

Tom and Ms. Martha show up right at 6. Just as everything is ready. Becky lets the two in and introduces everyone to each other. "Tom this is my best friend and co-worker, Lisa George. Lisa, this is Tom. He is the pastor, and this is Ms. Martha Gracie." Seeing something in Tom's eye, she adds, "Lisa wanted to be a part of our Bible study. I hope you don't mind."

"No, not at all. The more the merrier," Tom says with a big smile.

They all say, "Hello," and shake hands.

"I'm glad you don't mind that I invited Lisa." Becky says, but still feels there is something Tom's not saying. Then she dismisses it as her imagination.

"I hope you guys don't mind spaghetti." Becky says as she puts the food on the table.

"Yum, smells great, I love spaghetti." Martha says.

They sit down and eat, everyone compliments Becky on the food and Lisa even surprises Becky by bringing dessert. Tom and Martha brought a bottle of cola. And they have a good time eating and talking. By 6:45 dinner is over, and between the three women the table is cleared off and the dishes put in the dishwasher in no time. Becky says "The dishwasher is a bit noisy, I'll turn it on later." They all gather around the table again and Tom begins by giving a brief summery as to where they are in the Bible study, mostly for Lisa's benefit.

"So now we are about to learn more about the forth commandment . "**Exodus 20:8-11 Remember the Sabbath day, to keep it holy. 9. Six days you shall labor and do all your work, 10. but the seventh day is the Sabbath of the LORD your God. In it you shall do no work: you, nor your son, nor your daughter, nor your male servant, nor your female servant, nor your cattle, nor your stranger who is within your gates. 11. For in six days the LORD made the heavens and the earth, the sea, and all that is in them, and rested the seventh day. Therefore the LORD blessed the Sabbath day and hallowed it.**

"According to the calendar the seventh day is Saturday. The Spanish language calls Saturday Sábado or Sabbath." Tom informs the group. "I think all Christian churches will agree it is wrong to steal or lie or murder. There is only one commandment of the ten that the mainstream churches want to think has been 'done away with' and that's the fourth one, if not done away with at least changed to Sunday. The ones that feel the ten commandments are not done away with think the apostles changed the Sabbath to the first day of the week to honor Jesus and the day he was resurrected. They cite the time in **Acts 20: 7** when Paul spoke. They claim this proves the disciples meet on the first day of the week instead of the seventh. Martha will you read this account in Acts for us."

"Sure," Martha says and reads. "**Acts 20:7 Now on the first day of the week, when the disciples came together to break bread, Paul, ready to depart the next day, spoke to them and continued his message until midnight.** Shall I read more?"

"No, I think that's enough for now, thank you. " Tom says. "Let's dissect this verse. In **Acts 20:6** it says they stayed in Troas seven days. Paul was to leave the next day. First we have to realize that the first day of the week, or Sunday, was, for the Jews, a work day like our Monday. To come together to 'break bread' means to eat a meal, usually the evening meal. So if Billy Graham comes to town, he is going to hold a crusade every night he is here. No matter what day it is. It's the same with this verse. Paul is a very famous follower of Jesus and will create a gathering anywhere he is, any day he is there. So the people went to work, came home, ate supper, then settled down to listen to Paul speak. There is nothing that indicates a change in the Sabbath. Also Paul preached well into the next day. No one claims Monday to be holy. So what does the Bible say about the Sabbath?"

Tom reads, "**Acts 13:14, 42, 44 But when they departed from Perga, they came to Antioch in Pisidia, and went into the synagogue on the Sabbath day and sat down. ... 42 So when the Jews went out of the synagogue, the Gentiles begged that these words might be preached to them the next Sabbath. ... 44 On the next Sabbath almost the whole city came together to hear the word of God.**

Acts 16:13 And on the Sabbath day we went out of the city to the riverside, where prayer was customarily made; and we sat down and spoke to the women who met there.

Acts 17:2 then Paul, as his manner was, went in unto them, and three Sabbath days reasoned with them out of the scriptures,

Acts 18:4 And he reasoned in the synagogue every Sabbath, and persuaded both Jews and Greeks.

As you can see the disciples made it a practice to go to the synagogue every Sabbath. This doesn't sound to me like they changed anything."

Lisa asked, "So when and how did it get changed? And by whom?"

"Good question," Tom says, "The catholic church actually brags that they changed it. Let's look it up."

They all read the web site:

Catholic Church Admits They Made the Change

How It Happened...

Yet for nearly 2,000 years now, millions of Christians have worshiped on Sunday. So was the Sabbath changed from the seventh to the first day of the week? Let's look at the "yes" now.

"The Son of Man is Lord also of the Sabbath" (Luke 6:5). Here Jesus staked His claim and forbade anyone to meddle with the Sabbath. Yet He knew there would be those who would claim the power to change God's Law. Through Daniel he warned of just such a man. Describing a "little horn power" (Daniel 7:8), Daniel says, "He will speak against the Most High and oppress his saints and try to change the set times and the laws" (Daniel 7:25). Paul made a similar prediction: "Don't let anyone deceive you in any way, for that day will not come until the rebellion occurs and the man of lawlessness is revealed, the man doomed to destruction. He will oppose and will exalt himself over everything that is called God, or is worshiped, so that he sets himself up in God's temple, proclaiming himself to be God" (2 Thessalonians 2:3, 4, 7).

"Paul warned that this blasphemy was already at work, and that it would come not from an outside influence, but from within the church (2 Thessalonians 2:7, Acts 20:28-30). Sure enough, not long after Paul's day, apostasy appeared in the church.

"About 100 years before Christianity, Egyptian Mithraists introduced the festival of Sunday, dedicated to worshiping the sun, into the Roman Empire. Later, as Christianity grew, church leaders wished to increase the numbers of the church. In order to make the gospel more attractive to non-Christians, pagan customs were incorporated into the church's ceremonies. The custom of Sunday worship was welcomed by Christians who desired

to differentiate themselves from the Jews, whom they hated because of the Jews' rejection of the Savior. The first day of the week began to be recognized as both a religious and civil holiday. By the end of the second century, Christians considered it sinful to work on Sunday.

"The Roman emperor Constantine, a former sun-worshiper, professed conversion to Christianity, though his subsequent actions suggest the 'conversion' was more of a political move than a genuine heart change. Constantine named himself Bishop of the Catholic Church and enacted the first civil law regarding Sunday observance in A.D. 321.

"On the venerable day of the sun let the magistrate and people residing in cities rest, and let all workshops be closed. In the country however, persons engaged in agricultural work may freely and lawfully continue their pursuits; because it often happens that another day is not so suitable for grain growing or for vine planting; lest by neglecting the proper moment for such operations the bounty of heaven should be lost. —Schaff's History of the Christian Church, vol. III, chap. 75.

"Note that Constantine's law did not even mention Sabbath but referred to the mandated rest day as "the venerable day of the sun." And how kind he was to allow people to observe it as it was convenient. Contrast this with God's command to observe the Sabbath "even during the plowing season and harvest" (Exodus 34:21)! Perhaps the church leaders noticed this laxity as well, for just four years later, in A.D. 325, Pope Sylvester officially named Sunday "the Lord's Day," and in A.D. 338, Eusebius, the

court bishop of Constantine, wrote, "All things whatsoever that it was the duty to do on the Sabbath (the seventh day of the week) we (Constantine, Eusebius, and other bishops) have transferred to the Lord's Day (the first day of the week) as more appropriately belonging to it."

"Instead of the humble lives of persecution and self-sacrifice led by the apostles, church leaders now exalted themselves to the place of God. "This is the spirit of the antichrist, which you have heard is coming and even now is already in the world" (1 John 4:3).

"The Catechism

"Recall the ceremony with which God made known His Law, containing the blessing of the seventh-day Sabbath, by which all humanity is to be judged. Contrast this with the unannounced, unnoticed anticlimax with which the church gradually adopted Sunday at the command of 'Christian' emperors and Roman bishops. And these freely admit that they made the change from Sabbath to Sunday.

"In the Convert's Catechism of Catholic Doctrine, we read:

"Q. Which is the Sabbath day?

"A. Saturday is the Sabbath day.

"Q. Why do we observe Sunday instead of Saturday?

"A. We observe Sunday instead of Saturday because the Catholic Church, in the Council of Laodicea, (AD 336) transferred the solemnity from Saturday to Sunday….

"Q. Why did the Catholic Church substitute Sunday for Saturday?

"A. The Church substituted Sunday for Saturday, because Christ rose from the dead on a Sunday, and the Holy Ghost descended upon the Apostles on a Sunday.

"Q. By what authority did the Church substitute Sunday for Saturday?

"A. The Church substituted Sunday for Saturday by the plenitude of that divine power which Jesus Christ bestowed upon her!

—Rev. Peter Geiermann, C.SS.R., (1946), p. 50.

"In Catholic Christian Instructed,

"Q. Has the [Catholic] church power to make any alterations in the commandments of God?

"A. ...Instead of the seventh day, and other festivals appointed by the old law, the church has prescribed the Sundays and holy days to be set apart for God's worship; and these we are now obliged to keep in consequence of God's commandment, instead of the ancient Sabbath.

—The Catholic Christian Instructed in the Sacraments, Sacrifices, Ceremonies, and Observances of the Church By Way of Question and Answer, RT Rev. Dr. Challoner, p. 204.

"In An Abridgment of the Christian Doctrine,

"Q. How prove you that the church hath power to command feasts and holy days?

"A. By the very act of changing the Sabbath into Sunday, which Protestants allow of; and therefore they

fondly contradict themselves, by keeping Sunday strictly, and breaking most other feasts commanded by the same church.

"Q. How prove you that?

"A. Because by keeping Sunday, they acknowledge the church's power to ordain feasts, and to command them under sin; and by not keeping the rest [of the feasts] by her commanded, they again deny, in fact, the same power.

–Rev. Henry Tuberville, D.D. (R.C.), (1833), page 58.

"In A Doctrinal Catechism,

"Q. Have you any other way of proving that the Church has power to institute festivals of precept?

"A. Had she not such power, she could not have done that in which all modern religionists agree with her. She could not have substituted the observance of Sunday the first day of the week, for the observance of Saturday the seventh day, a change for which there is no Scriptural authority.

–Rev. Stephen Keenan, (1851), p. 174.

"In the Catechism of the Council of Trent,

"The Church of God has thought it well to transfer the celebration and observance of the Sabbath to Sunday!

–p 402, second revised edition (English), 1937. (First published in 1566)

"In the Augsburg Confession,

"They [the Catholics] allege the Sabbath changed into Sunday, the Lord's day, contrary to the Decalogue, as it appears; neither is there any example more boasted of than the changing of the Sabbath day. Great, they say, is

the power and authority of the church, since it dispensed with one of the ten commandments.

—Art. 28.

"God warned that a blasphemous power would 'seek to change times and laws,' and the Catholic Church openly admits doing it, even boasts about it. In a sermon at the Council of Trent in 1562, the Archbishop of Reggia, Caspar del Fossa, claimed that the Catholic Church's whole authority is based upon the fact that they changed the Sabbath to Sunday. Does this not fulfill the prophecies of Daniel and Paul?

"'For centuries millions of Christians have gathered to worship God on the first day of the week. Graciously He has accepted this worship. He has poured out His blessings upon Christian people as they have sought to serve Him. However, as one searches the Scriptures, he is forced to recognize that Sunday is not a day of God's appointment... It has no foundation in Scripture, but has arisen entirely as a result of custom,' says Frank H. Yost, Ph.D. in The Early Christian Sabbath.

"Let us ask the question again: Was the Sabbath changed from the seventh day of the week to the first? The Bible is clear: 'And God blessed the seventh day and made it holy' (Genesis 2:3). 'Therefore the Lord blessed the Sabbath day and made it holy' (Exodus 20:11). If God intended for another day to become the Sabbath, He must have removed the blessing from the seventh day and placed it on the day which was to replace it. But when God bestows a blessing, it is forever. '...You, O Lord, have blessed it, and it will be blessed forever' (1 Chronicles 17:27). 'I have

received a command to bless; He has blessed, and I cannot change it' (Numbers 23:20). Your birthday, a memorial of your birth, can't be changed, though you may celebrate it on a different day. Neither can the Sabbath, a memorial of creation (Exodus 20:11), be changed, though some may celebrate it on a different day.

"God instructed Moses to construct the earthly sanctuary, all its furniture, and the ark according to 'the pattern' he was shown. (Exodus 25:9, 40) The ark was called the 'ark of the covenant'" (Numbers 10:33, Deuteronomy 10:8, Hebrews 9:4), and the 'ark of the testimony' (Exodus 25:22), because in it Moses placed the tablets of stone on which God wrote His Law. (Exodus 25:16, 31:18) John, in Revelation 11:19, describes the scene before him when 'the temple of God was opened in Heaven.' John saw the ark of the covenant in the heavenly sanctuary. David wrote, 'Your word, O Lord, is eternal; it stands firm in the heavens' (Psalm 119:89). It is safe to assume that God's Law remains, contained within the ark of the covenant in the heavenly sanctuary.

"When God says, 'The seventh day is the Sabbath of the Lord your God' (Exodus 20:10), that ends all controversy. We cannot change God's Word for our own convenience. 'But if serving the Lord seems undesirable to you, then choose for yourselves this day whom you will serve' (Joshua 24:15).

"- Emily Thomsen

"- See more at: http://www.sabbathtruth.com/free-resources/article-library/id/916/catholic-church-admits-they-made-the-change#sthash.OsWK6RWn.dpuf"

"Wow!" Lisa proclaims, "I had no idea."

Becky agrees, "I can't believe any God fearing Church would buy into this….stuff."

Lisa asks Tom, "Does this mean everyone that worships on Sunday is going to the other place?"

"I don't think so. People are being deceived. That's for sure. But God is Love and I think he will correct them when He feels they are ready to be corrected. **We are saved by faith and not by works lest any man shall boast.** We aren't saved by the Law but by grace," Tom says.

Lisa says, "Wait now I'm confused. Are we to keep the Law of God or not?"

Becky looks at Tom in agreement with Lisa.

Tom answers, "Yes, we are to keep the Law. Let me explain. Sin is breaking the Law. Once we become a Christian we are dead to sin, so we are not to keep sinning. The thing is we don't keep the law to be saved, we keep the law because we are saved."

Martha breaks in, "Shall I read the scriptures that go along with what you are saying?"

"Yes, please," Tom says. Lisa and Becky look at Martha.

She reads, **"Ephesians 2:1, 8-10, 22 And you He made alive, who were dead in trespasses and sins, ... 8 For by grace you have been saved through faith, and that not of yourselves; it is the gift of God, 9 not of works, lest anyone should boast. 10 For we are His workmanship, created in Christ Jesus for good works,** (keeping Gods laws)

which God prepared beforehand that we should walk in them. (Gods Laws)**... 22 in whom you also are being built together for a dwelling place of God in the Spirit.**

Romans 5:1, 8-10, 13, 15, 20-21 Therefore, having been justified by faith, we have peace with God through our Lord Jesus Christ, ... 8 But God demonstrates His own love toward us, in that while we were still sinners, Christ died for us. 9 Much more then, having now been justified by His blood, we shall be saved from wrath through Him. 10 For if when we were enemies we were reconciled to God through the death of His Son, much more, having been reconciled, we shall be saved by His life. ... 13 For until the law sin was in the world, but sin is not imputed when there is no law. ... 15 But the free gift is not like the offense. For if by the one man's offense many died, much more the grace of God and the gift by the grace of the one Man, Jesus Christ, abounded to many. ... 20 Moreover the law entered that the offense might abound. But where sin abounded, grace abounded much more, 21 so that as sin reigned in death, even so grace might reign through righteousness to eternal life through Jesus Christ our Lord. Romans 6:1-23 What shall we say then? Shall we continue in sin that grace may abound? 2 <u>Certainly not</u>! How shall we who died to sin live any longer in it? 3 Or do you not know that as many of us as were baptized into Christ Jesus were baptized into His death? 4 Therefore we were buried with Him through baptism into death, that just as Christ was raised from the dead by the glory of the Father, even so we also should walk in newness of life. 5 For if we have been united together in the likeness

of His death, certainly we also shall be in the likeness of
His resurrection, 6 knowing this, that our old man was
crucified with Him, that the body of sin might be done
away with, that we should no longer be slaves of sin. 7
For he who has died has been freed from sin. 8 Now if we
died with Christ, we believe that we shall also live with
Him, 9 knowing that Christ, having been raised from
the dead, dies no more. Death no longer has dominion
over Him. 10 For the death that He died, He died to
sin once for all; but the life that He lives, He lives to
God. 11 Likewise you also, reckon yourselves to be dead
indeed to sin, but alive to God in Christ Jesus our Lord.
12 Therefore do not let sin reign in your mortal body,
that you should obey it in its lusts. 13 And do not present
your members as instruments of unrighteousness to sin,
but present yourselves to God as being alive from the
dead, and your members as instruments of righteousness
to God. 14 For sin shall not have dominion over you, for
you are not under law but under grace. 15 What then?
Shall we sin because we are not under law but under
grace? Certainly not! 16 Do you not know that to whom
you present yourselves slaves to obey, you are that one's
slaves whom you obey, whether of sin leading to death,
or of obedience leading to righteousness? 17 But God
be thanked that though you were slaves of sin, yet you
obeyed from the heart that form of doctrine to which
you were delivered. 18 And having been set free from sin,
you became slaves of righteousness. 19 I speak in human
terms because of the weakness of your flesh. For just as
you presented your members as slaves of uncleanness, and

of lawlessness leading to more lawlessness, so now present your members as slaves of righteousness for holiness. 20 For when you were slaves of sin, you were free in regard to righteousness. 21 What fruit did you have then in the things of which you are now ashamed? For the end of those things is death. 22 But now having been set free from sin, and having become slaves of God, you have your fruit to holiness, and the end, everlasting life. 23 For the wages of sin is death, but the gift of God is eternal life in Christ Jesus our Lord.

All of that basically says what Tom said We don't keep the Law to be saved but we keep the Law because we are saved. Let me also read:" Martha continues.

"James 2:1, 8-24, 26 My brethren, do not hold the faith of our Lord Jesus Christ, the Lord of glory, with partiality. ... 8 If you really fulfill the royal law according to the Scripture, 'You shall love your neighbor as yourself,' you do well; 9 but if you show partiality, you commit sin, and are convicted by the law as transgressors. 10 For whoever shall keep the whole law, and yet stumble in one point, he is guilty of all. 11 For He who said, 'Do not commit adultery,' also said, 'Do not murder.' Now if you do not commit adultery, but you do murder, you have become a transgressor of the law. 12 So whatever you say or whatever you do, remember that you will be judged by the law that sets you free. 13 There will be no mercy for those who have not shown mercy to others. But if you have been merciful, God will be merciful when he judges you. 14 What good is it, dear brothers and sisters, if you say you have faith but don't show it by your actions? Can that

kind of faith save anyone? 15 If a brother or sister is naked and destitute of daily food, 16 and one of you says to them, 'Depart in peace, be warmed and filled,' but you do not give them the things which are needed for the body, what does it profit? 17 Thus also faith by itself, if it does not have works, is dead. 18 But someone will say, 'You have faith, and I have works.' Show me your faith without your works, and I will show you my faith by my works. 19 You believe that there is one God. You do well. Even the demons believe--and tremble! 20 But do you want to know, O foolish man, that faith without works is dead? 21 Was not Abraham our father justified by works when he offered Isaac his son on the altar? 22 Do you see that faith was working together with his works, and by works faith was made perfect? 23 And the Scripture was fulfilled which says, 'Abraham believed God, and it was accounted to him for righteousness.' And he was called the friend of God. 24 You see then that a man is justified by works, and not by faith only. ... 26 For as the body without the spirit is dead, so faith without works is dead also.

Good works include; Studying and Keeping all of Gods laws as best we can, and helping our brothers in any way we can, physically, mentally, and emotionally. by giving our time, our caring, and our money whenever and wherever we can, Basically giving of ourselves to God first and then to our fellow man. That includes our families. We are to be a living sacrifice of love in that way," Martha finishes and sits back.

"Ok, I see," Becky says, " In the old testament they tried to keep the Law of God thinking that would save them, but even then it took a belief in the coming Christ to truly save them. Then after Jesus came we now look both behind at his first coming and ahead to his second coming, and believe in him to be saved, We are now under the Law of Love, but we still need the Law of God to show us how to love."

"Exactly," Tom says, "The mainstream Christians think that Sabbath was changed to Sunday to honor Jesus. And they are totally convinced of that. But worshiping Jesus in that way violates the first commandment of '**You shall have no other gods before me.**' And the third one that says, '**You shall not take the Lords name in vain.'** If you say you belong to God the father but only worship the Son by keeping Sunday you take Gods name in vain."

"Oh," Lisa says thoughtfully, "I'm so glad I came tonight. This has been a real eye opener."

"Lisa," Martha asks, "What's your story? Are you a Christian?"

"Oh, yes, my parents are Baptists and, of course, they raised me as a Baptist," Lisa explains," But lately we have, I have fallen away from going to church. I guess I got too busy and, well, church just isn't doing 'it' for me, too much fire and brimstone and not enough love. But your church sounds like just what I've been looking for. A church that emphasizes the love of God and Jesus, not the scary stuff. I'm anxious to learn more, but it's getting late and I have to get home. When is the next Bible study going to happen?"

"How about tomorrow," Becky suggests.

"Oh, sorry. I can't tomorrow. I have to take my daughter to her ballet class," Lisa says.

Becky states, "I didn't know Elisa took ballet."

"Yes, since she was three," Lisa explains.

Martha asks, "How old is she now?"

"She is eight," Lisa says.

"Samantha is nine, that's another family in the church's daughter. I know she would love to meet someone her own age," Martha says.

"That sounds great, I'll be sure to bring her when I come to church next Sabbath. That sounds a little weird to say," Lisa confesses.

Martha reassures her, "You'll get use to it. Soon it will seem like you've been saying Sabbath all your life."

Tom pipes up and says, "So we will be seeing you at church next Saturday then?"

"Oh, yes, after learning what I've learned here tonight. I definitely believe in a Saturday Sabbath. I don't want to follow the Catholic decrees any more. I'm definitely not Catholic," Lisa states emphatically. "I'm sure Becky won't mind giving us a ride at least for the first time, so I can learn the way and all?" Lisa says as she looks at Becky with pleading in her eyes.

"Of course I will give you a ride. Happy to do that, it will be fun. What about Wednesday? Can we meet here Wednesday for more study?" Becky asks.

Tom says, "Ok by me. What about the rest of you?"

Martha says. "I'm good with that. What about you, Lisa? Is that good for you?"

Lisa checks her little notebook she keeps in her purse and says, "That's fine with me, I'm actually open that night. But the rest of the week is booked until Saturday."

Martha says, "Ok, but we will bring the food next time. Don't want Becky having to do it all, all of the time."

Becky says, "I don't mind….but if you insist we could make it a pot luck like at church."

Martha says, "Ok, but I'm bringing the main dish, the rest of you can bring the sides."

"I'll bring drinks," Tom says.

Lisa adds, "I'll bring dessert. That's what I'm good at."

Becky says, "That leaves me with the salad. My specialty."

"Great, we're all set then," Martha says, as they all file out the door. "See you all on Wednesday."

Becky shuts the door behind them, and smiles to herself. Then she heads to her bedroom to get ready for bed.

-6-

Wednesday evening comes quickly and soon all the new friends are gathered in Becky's apartment. Becky's "Berry and nut on greens" salad is a hit. Tom brings bottles of alcohol free sparkling apple juice. Martha's meatless meat loaf is so good Lisa doesn't even know it is meatless. Clara, Martha's sister comes along too and brings her home-grown green beans. Lastly Lisa brings, home-made cheese cake. Every one eats until they can't eat any more. Becky is happy Clara has come too. She was hoping to get to know the quiet regal lady better. Martha and Clara, though they look alike, are very different. Martha is out-going and a social butterfly. Clara is quiet and keeps to herself, but is extremely intelligent and amazing to talk to.

The group settles in around the now cleared table. Tom starts with a question. "Lisa or Becky, do either of you have a particular question you would like to have answered?

Lisa says, "I have a lot of questions, but I guess the first one is how did you come up with when the day begins? Becky told me you guys believe the day begins and ends at sundown. That seems so weird to me. I can understand sunrise to sunrise, but to begin the day at the end of the day sees, well,....crazy to me."

Tom smiles and Martha giggles just a bit, but it is Clara that answers the question.

"I had a hard time accepting this myself. I read the account in Genesis, but it still didn't make sense. Lets read it first. **Genesis 1:1-5 In the beginning God created the heavens and the earth. 2 The earth was without form, and void; and darkness was on the face of the deep. And the Spirit of God was hovering over the face of the waters. 3 Then God said, 'Let there be light'; and there was light. 4 And God saw the light, that it was good; and God divided the light from the darkness. 5 God called the light Day, and the darkness He called Night. <u>So the evening and the morning were the first day.</u>**

"What I wrestled with was that first night lasted for a very long time. So how could God say the evening and the morning were the first day? It really seemed like it should be the morning and the evening would be the first day. But then I realized that God had to start creating the world as we know it, in the dark for that was all there was. Since he began working in the dark that is where he declared the day would begin."

Lisa thinks about this for a minute, then says," I guess that makes sense."

Becky adds, "I guess I never thought about it one way or the other. It sure can make things confusing though. If someone says I'll meet you Monday night does that mean they want to meet you at sundown Sunday or sundown Monday?"

Lisa speaks up and asks, "What does it matter anyway?"

Tom answers, " Since we live in a world where the day begins at midnight and that is what we are use to, I think it is ok to continue to think and count the days that way. Until it comes to the Sabbath and the Holy days. Then we should honor God and count it from sundown to sundown as He intended."

"The Sabbath first began in Genesis," Clara interjects. "Let me read it, **Genesis 2:1-3 Thus the heavens and the earth, and all the host of them, were finished. 2 And on the seventh day God ended His work which He had done, and He rested on the seventh day from all His work which He had done. 3 Then God blessed the seventh day and sanctified it, because in it He rested from all His work which God had created and made."**

Becky says, "I didn't realize the Sabbath started at creation. So I guess that means the Sabbath isn't just for the Jews but for all people."

Martha states, "That's what we believe."

Lisa says, "That's what I believe too… now."

"Is there anything else either of you wants to know before we call it a night?" Tom asks.

"All of this is so different from what I was taught. I don't know where you will go next' or what else you are going to reveal to me that I didn't know. I'm afraid I don't know enough to know what to ask," Lisa states.

"Well, I have a question, two actually. Tom, a while back you mentioned 613 Biblical Laws. We covered ten of them. What about the other 603 laws? " Becky asks.

"That's a good question," Tom says. "but I'm afraid it will have to wait till next time. We don't have enough time to cover them now."

"Ok, next time, but what about those Holy days you mentioned? Is that like Christmas and Easter? Or are you talking about something else?

Tom states, "There are seven maybe eight depending on how you look at it. There's the spring Holy days, two for Passover the first day and the last day, and some people count first fruits as a holy day, even though the Bible doesn't expressly call it a Holy Day. It does mention what we are to do on that day. Then there is one fifty days later called Pentecost."

Lisa jumps in with, "I've heard of Pentecost. There's a whole church called the Pentecostal Church. They speak in tongues. A bit too weird for me. Even though I've never actually been to a Pentecostal church. I don't think I would want to go either."

"Yes, there is a Pentecostal Church, and the Bible does talk about speaking in tongues, or unknown languages, but the Bible also has specific rules for speaking in tongues found in **1st Corinthians 14**, but I don't think they follow them, at least not in my experience," Clara says.

Tom says, " Yes, this too we will cover later. Let's continue with the list of Holy Days. There are four holy days in the fall. Trumpets, Atonement, and the Feast of Tabernacles, with the first and last day being holy. These are also a part of the 603 laws of God we still have to cover. Again we don't have time now to go into them, I'm afraid we took too much time eating that delicious supper," Tom smiles at the thought of all the good food they had just eaten not long ago.

"That's ok, Sabbath will be here before we know it. I'm looking forward to it," Becky says.

Lisa adds, "Yes, me too. I can hardly wait. Well, I'll see you at work tomorrow Becky," as she heads out the door.

"Ok, see you," Becky says to Lisa. "I will see the rest of you on Sabbath. And It was such a pleasure to get to know you a little better, Ms. Clara."

"Thank you, dear," Clara says, "I'll see you and Lisa on Sabbath then."

"Yes, goodbye for now," Becky says as the group leaves her apartment and she shuts the door.

Thursday Lisa and Becky talk about Sabbath. Lisa tells Becky that she can't come for vespers Friday night, but she and Elisa will be ready to go first thing Sabbath morning.

"Great," Becky says. The rest of the work day goes by uneventfully.

After work Becky pulls into the parking lot of her apartment building, parks in her usual place, then walks the short distance to the communal mail boxes to get her mail. There is a lady there getting her mail. When she looks up, Becky sees it is the lady who offered her a ride home from the other church a couple of weeks ago.

"Hi, Becky, right? I didn't know you lived in this apartment building. I guess we are going to be neighbors. We just moved in this week. I would say we could all ride to church together, but I'm afraid due to circumstances beyond our control we won't be going to church. Jeff, my Husband, got a great promotion, but that means he has to work on Sundays. He gets Friday and Saturday off now. I guess I could go to church without him, but that wouldn't feel right, He really enjoys going to church. I just can't go without him," the lady says.

"I wish we could find a church that meets on Saturday, but I guess that is wishful thinking."

"You could come to the church I'm going to now. We meet on Sa…, um, Saturday," Becky says.

"Really, there really is a church that meets on Saturday?" the young lady asks.

"Yes," Becky states. "I'm sorry, I don't remember your name."

"Oh, I'm sorry. It's Crystal, Crystal Longley, Jeff and Crystal Longley. A Saturday keeping church. It's not Jewish is it?" Crystal asks a bit alarmed.

"No, it's Christian," Becky reassures her.

"Wow, I'll tell Jeff about it and see if he wants to try it out." Crystal says as she heads off to her own apartment. "What time?" She yells back over her shoulder.

"I don't know exactly, kind of early 8 or 9-ish, I would guess," Becky says to the retreating Crystal.

Crystal half shouts back, "Ok," as she waves good bye.

Becky smiles, and says to herself. "Wow, I've only gone to this new church once and I've already got two other families interested in going too. It must be a sign that this is where God wants me to be."

Friday nothing seems to be going right for Becky. First her boss yells at her for no reason. then she has to stay late. Lisa has taken the day off, so Becky has to do her work too. Then it's payday and she has to go grocery shopping. She figures she will be missing Vespers also, and she really wanted to go. As she is intently looking for what she wants at the store, she hears someone call her name. She looks around to see the pastor of the church she went to before she found the Sabbath church.

"Oh, hi, Pastor," Becky says in a friendly voice.

"Hi, Becky, I thought you had dropped off the face of the earth. We've missed you at church. Can we expect to see you this Sunday?" Pastor Nickels asks.

"I'm sorry, probably not, well, no, actually." Becky says. She really doesn't want to get into it with him right now. She is in a hurry to get home before dark. If she hurries she might make some of the service. But Pastor Nickels isn't going to let her off so fast.

"You're not? I must know why?" he says.

Becky sighs and says, "I've been going to a Sabbath keeping church. We meet on Saturday."

"You haven't turned Jewish on us, have you?" Pastor asks with concern in his voice.

"No, it's a Christian church. We just believe in the fourth commandment of remembering the Sabbath Day. That's all," Becky explains.

Pastor Nickels, now a little irritated, says, "You know we aren't under the old testament laws anymore. Jesus did away with them. They were hung on the cross. We are under the free gift of grace now. Why would you want to go back to that system' when it couldn't save anyone. You are turning your back on everything Jesus ever did. You are a Jew. It was the Jews that killed our Lord in the first place. And now you honor them? No, you're not a Jew. You are worse than a Jew, you're a hypocrite. You better come back to the true church before it's too late. You'll end up in Hades for sure." By now he is really worked up and mad. He looks at Becky in a way that really scares her, then he slams down the pork roast he was carrying and storms out the door. Everyone in the store is staring at Becky. A very nice lady asks Becky if she is alright?

Becky nods, "He didn't even give me a chance to explain," she says visibly shaken up.

"It will be ok, dear. Let's get these groceries paid for. You go home and relax. Everything will work out. You'll see. Things will be brighter in the morning." The kind lady heads the now in shock Becky to the checkout counter and even pays for her meager supply of groceries. By the time the nice lady gets Becky to her car tears are starting to well up in Becky's eyes.

"Are you going to be ok driving home, dear?" the lady asks.

Becky recomposes herself and says' "Yes, thank you so much' you've been a real Godsend. I'll be fine. What do I owe you for the groceries?"

"Oh, dear, no, they're on me. You've been through enough tonight. Besides you didn't get very much." The kind lady says. "You can pay for someone else one day." At that the kind lady leaves. Becky feels bad she didn't even get the lady's name. She will have to get Tom to say a prayer for her tomorrow. Oh, no, Tom, Church. I really need to talk to Tom. It's already dark. They are probably all gone from the church. But Becky heads there anyway hoping and praying Tom is still there. Half way to church anger kicks in and she starts yelling in the car.

"How dare him attack me like that. He is such a creep. He'll never see me in that church again." She rants and raves all the way to the church.

She gets to the church just in time, Tom is just locking up to go home. "Becky? Are you alright? You look…upset. What happened?" He asks as he gets in her car in the passenger's side.

"I… I'm so upset I don't even know where to begin," Becky confesses.

"Are you ok?" Tom asks with concern.

"Yes, I wasn't mugged or anything. I just had an upsetting encounter with the Pastor of the Sunday church. I only went there once. The nerve of him to treat me that way." Becky is starting to get riled up again.

Tom calmly says, "Ok, take a big breath, start at the beginning and tell me everything that happened."

Becky takes a calming breath and starts in. "First my boss jumps all over me for something I didn't do. Then because Lisa took the day off, I had to stay late and do her work. I don't blame Lisa for taking the day off, she deserves it, but they could have told me I had to do her work, before the last minute in the day. If I had known, I would have done it earlier in the day. Then I had to go to the store. I was totally out of groceries. So while I'm there trying to hurry so I can at least get in some of the service here, Pastor Nickels sees me and wants to know why,… No demands to know why, I haven't come to church. I tried to be diplomatic but he has to have all the details. So I told him I was coming here to church now. And he exploded and accused me of living under the law and being worse than a Jew, and that I was going to go to Hades. It was awful. I felt hurt, and violated, and stunned and then mad, very mad. Even now just talking about it I'm getting mad all over again." Becky takes a breath, "If it hadn't been for the 'good Samaritan' lad, I don't know what I would have done."

"What good Samaritan lady," Tom asks.

"Oh, she was an angel, she took my stunned self under her wing, bought my groceries, and made sure I got to my car ok. I think she would have driven me home if I had asked her to." Becky smiles at the memory. "I didn't even get her name, but I would love to ask God to bless her."

"God knows who she is. I think he put her there just at the right time to help you when you needed it," Tom says.

They sit quiet for a moment then Becky asks, "Was he right? Am I being a hypocrite?"

Tom says, "No, remember all that you have learned so far. We are trying to be the best we can be to please our Father, not impress him with how 'good' we are."

"Yes, I remember, that's what I thought. So why would a man that is suppose to know the Bible jump all over me like that. It doesn't make sense," Becky says.

"I don't know. Sometimes God allows us to be tested. To see how we will react, whether we will take the road of love or hate. God asks us to love our enemies and to pray for them." Tom looks Becky in the eye and continues, "It's ok to get mad. Even Jesus got mad, but we need to learn how to get mad and still not sin. ....What are you going to do?" Tom asks as he looks at her.

"I don't know, what should I do?" Becky asks.

Tom still looking at her says."That is up to you, that is what free will is all about."

"Ok, what would you do?" Becky asks, getting a bit frustrated.

Tom answers with, "Well, the old me would get mad and ask God to curse him somehow, then I would go about trying to ruin him, but that was the old me. Now I would forgive him for what he did, because he doesn't know what he is doing, like Christ asked God to forgive the people for crucifying him. Because they didn't know what they were doing. Then I would ask God to bless him and open his heart and his eyes to the truth," Tom explains.

Becky lowers her head and says, "I think that is what God would want me to do and that is what I want to do. I want to do what's right. I want to ask God to forgive me for getting mad and wanting to hurt him the way he hurt me. Then I want to ask God to bless him and open his eyes and heart like you said." She looks at Tom and her eyes plead for help.

Tom reaches over and squeezes her hand, "Ok, I'll start a prayer but I hope you will finish it." Tom prays, "Daddy, Becky has been through a lot tonight and has learned a valuable lesson about your love, and your will for her. I ask that you forgive Pastor Nickels and bless him with whatever he needs. He sounds like a man in need. And bless Becky for acknowledging her weakness and wanting to become more like you in everything she does. Amen." Tom sets with his head bowed waiting to see if Becky will add anything to the prayer. He is about to look up when he hears her small voice crack and say. "God, I thank you for your help tonight, for showing me the right way to respond to threats from the enemy. I thank you for sending the angel lady to help me and whoever she is, please give her a special blessing. Help me to remember her kindness and pass that kindness on to others. And bless Pastor Nickels that he might grow in your truth and knowledge. Amen." Becky looks up with tears in her eyes, but this time they are not tears of pain or anger or frustration, but tears of overwhelming thankfulness and love. She wipes her eyes and smiles at Tom, then gives him a hug.

"Feel better?" Tom asks.

Becky nods and smiles again. "Better than ever," she says.

"Good, I'll see you tomorrow then," Tom says as he exits the car.

Becky drives home and unloads her car. It then hits her that she only got about a fourth of what she needed from the store. This strikes her as being very funny and she laughs out loud. If the neighbors could hear her they would probably think she was totally nuts and she laughs even harder. She is still giggling as she crawls into bed.

She sleeps later then she had planned to. And when through sleepy eyes she sees the time, she jumps out of bed and is hit by a moment of sheer panic. But calms down quickly. She goes into her bathroom, showers, and gets dressed. As she is coming out of her room there is a knock at her door. She figures it's Lisa and Elisa and opens the door to find Crystal and Jeff standing there. "Hi," Becky says surprised, "Come in. Are you here to go to church?"

"Yes, if that's ok?" Crystal says. Crystal and Jeff are around Becky's age. Crystal is very energetic and outgoing. Jeff is quiet and laid back. They both have a contagious light about them. Becky thinks, "*you just can't help but like these two.*"

Then Becky realizes she never told Crystal which apartment was hers. So she asks, "Crystal, how did you know which apartment is mine?"

"That was easy, our apartment numbers are on our mailboxes. I just looked at the one you had opened." Crystal says like it was no big deal.

Jeff says, "Crystal has a photographic memory. If she sees it, or hears it, it's in her mind forever."

"Not forever," Crystal says, "I could forget things if I wanted too. I just don't want too." She giggles and flutters away.

"What time does church start," Jeff asks.

"I'm not sure, I guess whenever we get there," Becky says.

Jeff looks puzzled. "What kind of church is this, that they don't have a start time?"

"They don't have an end time ether." Becky says, "Church lasts all day and people just sort of come and go, mostly come, all day long."

"Interesting," Jeff says. "So what are we waiting for?"

"I have two more friends coming, they should be here soon. Oh, and they serve breakfast at church too," Becky says, just as the door bell rings.

"That's good, I'm starved," Crystal says as Becky answers the door and invites Lisa and Elisa in.

"Lisa this is Jeff and Crystal Longley. They are my new neighbors. Crystal and Jeff, this is Lisa George and her daughter Elisa. Lisa and I work together. Jeff and Crystal want to go to church with us today too," Becky explains.

Lisa lightens up at this news and says, "Great, the more the merrier. I'm excited to get to know the two of you."

Jeff says "My van is big enough for all of us if we all want to go together."

"Sure, that will be fun." Lisa and Becky say together. The group all head out to the parking lot, and Becky locks her door. They all pile into Jeff's van. Jeff asks Becky to sit up front so she can tell him the way. In just a few minutes Becky announces,

"Here we are."

Jeff says "Here? This is just a house. Are you sure this is it?"

"Yes, I'm sure." Becky says. "Just pull into the backyard and park at the fence."

Jeff does as instructed, and they all pile out. There are two other cars in the yard. Becky recognizes Tom's car and she thinks the other car is Martha's.

The group goes into the main room of the church, where they meet Tom.

Becky introduces everyone, "Hi, Tom, you remember Lisa. This is her daughter, Elisa, and this is Jeff and Crystal Longley. They just moved in to my apartment complex. They wanted to come see what this church was like. Everybody, this is Tom, he is the pastor of this little congregation."

"Hi, everyone, and welcome to the Lord of the Sabbath Church. It's wonderful that you have all come today. I'm looking forward to getting to know all of you better," Tom says enthusiastically.

The group says, "Hi, Tom," in unison.

Martha, Clara, and Ms. Carcie, are here as well. They also are introduced to each other. Lisa asks, "Where is the restroom?" Martha quickly shows Lisa and Elisa where the restroom is, and the two head off.

"Breakfast will be ready soon. The others should be coming along shortly," Martha says as she comes out of the kitchen, drying her hands on a towel.

Pat and Rachel show up next, Becky introduces them to her friends. It doesn't take long before Pat and Jeff find a quiet corner so Jeff can get some questions answered. They seem to hit it off very well.

Becky is floored when Crystal and Rachel and she are talking and Rachel mentions she is pregnant, and Crystal says, "Me too". They are both three months pregnant and both couples have been married for a year. Soon Crystal and Rachel are off talking baby stuff. A subject Becky can't really relate to since she doesn't even have a boyfriend, let alone a husband or kids.

The Wilsons show up next and almost instantly Samantha and Elisa are acting as though they have known each other forever.

Lisa tells Becky, "This is terrific, Elisa and Samantha go to the same school. Elisa has always thought Sam was a fantastic girl and has wanted to get to know her better, but school always seems to get in the way, so now they can get to know each other without the interference of everything else."

Lisa goes off to talk to Julie and leaves Becky to fend for herself.

A new family shows up that Becky hasn't meet yet. They are the Dawn family. Valerie and Michael and their two sons Jayden 11, and Ethan 6.

Becky sits down and thinks, "*Everyone has someone to hang with except me. Even JJ and Charlie have Jayden and Ethan to play with.*" She is happy her friends are making new friends and getting comfortable with this new church, but she is also new to this church and right now she is feeling a bit left out.

Becky is deep in thought when she hears a gravelly voice behind her, "Feeling a bit left out, dear?" Becky jumps and turns around to see Ms. Marcie behind her. "Oh, I'm sorry, I didn't see you there."

"That's ok, I can see you are deep in your own mind. Feeling happy for your friends and sad for yourself all at the same time," Ms. Marcie says. "But you're not alone, Jesus is always by you, around you, and inside you. You should never feel alone."

Becky smiles and says, "Yes, you are right. Thank you, Ms. Marcie. You are so very wise."

Lisa slides in beside Becky at this time, gives Becky a hug, and says, "This is great, Elisa is getting to know Samantha, Elisa looks up to Sam, she is very popular. And now I get to know Julie too. I'm so glad you brought us here. Thank you."

Lisa sits by Becky and Ms. Marcie for the rest of the breakfast. The three talk about the church, and life, and everything, while they eat veggie Bacon, farm fresh eggs, and homemade biscuits.

After breakfast, everyone breaks up into Sabbath School classes.

The kids all go to their age group classes with their teachers.

Tom, Pat, and Jeff go to one room and Becky, Lisa, Crystal, Martha and Rachel go to another room. The others all go to their usual classes.

Martha starts, "After Becky started coming, we decided we needed a beginners class or new women's class. So I'm delighted to see we have not just one but three new ladies in our class today."

Rachel adds, "We thought we would keep this rather informal and let you guys ask questions and we will discover the answers together. Sound ok with everyone?"

"Ooh, I like that idea," Lisa says. Becky smiles and nods in agreement. Crystal, starting to look a little bored, shrugs her shoulders and says, "That's ok with me."

"So does anyone have a question?" Martha asks.

Crystal says, "No," and looks away.

Becky says, "Yes, I have a question. Tom said something about 613 Biblical laws. We have covered 10 of them. What about the other 603 laws?"

"That is a good question," Martha says.

Lisa asks, "Are there any laws that have been done away with'?"

Martha states, "Let me first state that God's laws are God's laws. And just as God does not change, his laws do not change. They are what they are. But cultures do change. We have things now that they didn't have then. Like refrigerators, and stoves, and cars. And we are not all farmers like they were then. We have cities and different countries and each of them have their own rules and laws. The Bible says that we are to honor our rulers and that we are not to take the law into our own hands. That's why we have police and lawyers and judges, etcetera. But if and some day when the countries' laws go blatantly against God's laws then we will have to defy our rulers and choose God over everything else, even over our own life. But we will get into that later."

"I think we should start with the laws on sacrifices," Rachel suggests.

"Ok," Martha says, "According to the list there are 102 laws concerning sacrifices and burnt offerings. Lets first see what the new testament says." Martha reads the following: **"Ephesians 5:2 NKJV And walk in love, as Christ also has loved us and given Himself for us, an offering and a sacrifice to God for a sweet-smelling aroma.**

Hebrews 10:1, 4, 10, 12, 14, 19-20 For the law, having a shadow of the good things to come, and not the very image of the things, can never with these same sacrifices, which they offer continually year by year, make those who approach perfect. ... 4 For it is not possible that the blood of bulls and goats could take away sins. ... 10 By that will we have been sanctified through the offering of the body of Jesus Christ once for all. ... 12 But this Man, after He had offered one sacrifice for sins forever, sat down at the right hand of God, ... 14 For by one offering He has perfected forever those who are being sanctified. ... 19 Therefore, brethren, having boldness to enter the Holiest by the blood of Jesus, 20 by a new and living way which He consecrated for us, through the veil, that is, His flesh,

Hebrews 13:15 Therefore by Him let us continually offer the sacrifice of praise to God, that is, the fruit of our lips, giving thanks to His name.

So we see that Jesus is our ultimate sacrifice eliminating the need for continually sacrificing animals for our sins. I think it is against our civil law to sacrifice animals nowadays anyway, " Martha finishes.

Rachel interjects, "But we do make a daily sacrifice. We are to sacrifice our will, our emotions or hearts, as the Bible puts it, to God daily, hourly if need be. We are a living sacrifice to God. **Romans 12:1 NKJV - 1 I beseech you therefore, brethren, by the mercies of God, that you present your bodies a living sacrifice, holy, acceptable to God, which is your reasonable service."**

Crystal stands up and says a bit huffily, "I don't like that version of the Bible it's too hard for me to understand." She sits down, defiantly frowning.

Martha, motherly says, "I'm sorry Crystal. There are more modern versions, we can use one of those if you would like?"

"Yes, please." Crystal says lightening up. "I like The New Living Translation."

"Is that alright with everyone?" Martha asks the group.

"That's fine with me," Lisa says.

"Me too," Becky says with a shrug.

Rachel puts her thoughts into it by saying, "I'm ok with it as long as we cross reference it with other versions when there is need to do so, to clarify the true meaning of a verse."

"That sounds good to me. So it's settled. We'll use the New Living Translation unless we have a need to clarify something," Martha states.

"So back to the point. The Bible states that animal sacrifices were introduced because of sin. And the remission of sin requires blood to eradicate it. Animals were used for two reasons. 1. God forbid human sacrifices, especially children, as the heathen would sacrifice their children to their gods which is really the devil. And 2. Animals never fell from grace so their blood is innocent blood. But the blood of animals can never really cleanse us from our sins, not permanently anyway. It can only cover up our sins. It took the blood of Jesus to fully cleanse us once and for all. Therefore the need to sacrifice animals no longer is needed. Jesus did that once and for all. So that eliminates 102 of the laws. Is that clear to everyone?"

Rachel says, "I would like to read in the Bible where it states what you said If you don't mind."

Martha says, "Yes, please."

Rachel reads, **"Genesis 3:17, 21, 23 NLT And to the man he said, "Since you listened to your wife and ate from the tree whose fruit I commanded you not to eat, the ground is cursed because of you. All your life you will struggle to scratch a living from it. ... 21 And the LORD God made clothing from animal skins for Adam and his wife. ...'** The first animal sacrifice." Rachel interjects. She reads on, **"23 So the LORD God banished them from the Garden of Eden, and he sent Adam out to cultivate the ground from which he had been made.**

"Jumping ahead in time we read," Rachel continues, **"Genesis 4:4, 7 NLT Abel also brought a gift--the best of the firstborn lambs from his flock. The LORD accepted Abel and his gift, ... 7 You will be accepted if you do what is right. But if you refuse to do what is right, then watch out! Sin is crouching at the door, eager to control you. But you must subdue it and be its master.**

Romans 5:17 For the sin of this one man, Adam, caused death to rule over all, But even greater is God's wonderful grace and his gift of righteousness, for all who receive it

will triumph over sin and death through this one man, Jesus Christ.

Hebrews 9:7-9 But only the high priest ever entered the Most Holy Place, and only once a year. And he always offered blood for his own sins and for the sins the people had committed in ignorance. 8 By these regulations the Holy Spirit revealed that the entrance to the Most Holy Place was not freely open as long as the Tabernacle and the system it represented were still in use. 9 This is an illustration pointing to the present time. For the gifts and sacrifices that the priests offer are not able to cleanse the consciences of the people who bring them.

Hebrews 9:14, 22-28 Just think how much more the blood of Christ will purify our consciences from sinful deeds so that we can worship the living God. For by the power of the eternal Spirit, Christ offered himself to God as a perfect sacrifice for our sins. ... 22 In fact, according to the law of Moses, nearly everything was purified with blood. For without the shedding of blood, there is no forgiveness. 23 That is why the Tabernacle and everything in it, which were copies of things in heaven, had to be purified by the blood of animals. But the real things in heaven had to be purified with far better sacrifices than the blood of animals. 24 For Christ did not enter into a holy place made with human hands, which was only a copy of the true one in heaven. He entered into heaven itself to appear now before God on our behalf. 25 And he did not enter heaven to offer himself again and again, like the high priest here on earth who enters the Most Holy Place year after year with the blood of an animal.

26 If that had been necessary, Christ would have had to die again and again, ever since the world began. But now, once for all time, he has appeared at the end of the age to remove sin by his own death as a sacrifice. 27 And just as each person is destined to die once and after that comes judgment, 28 so also Christ died once for all time as a sacrifice to take away the sins of many people. He will come again, not to deal with our sins, but to bring salvation to all who are eagerly waiting for him."

"'Thank you Rachel," Martha says. "Are we ready to proceed?"

"Yes," they all say.

Rachel says, "I have been looking at this supposed 'list' of laws on the internet. I find that they jump around a lot and are quite often redundant. I also find that some of the 'laws' are not what they say they are. I propose we just read the Bible where the laws come from and make up our own minds as to how relevant they are."

"That sounds good to me," Becky says, and they all agree.

Martha says, "I guess the best place to start is Genesis. Rachel do you know of any laws that are in Genesis?"

Rachel says, " There are a few mentioned in Genesis but most of them are in Exodus, Leviticus, and Deuteronomy. There is Genesis 17:12 and it is repeated in Leviticus 12:3."

Rachel reads, "**Genesis 17:9 NLT - 9 Then God said to Abraham, 'Your responsibility is to obey the terms of the covenant. You and all your descendants have this continual responsibility. 10 This is the covenant that you and your descendants must keep: Each male among you must be circumcised… 12 From generation to generation,**

every male child must be circumcised on the eighth day after his birth. This applies not only to members of your family but also to the servants born in your household and the foreign-born servants whom you have purchased.

Leviticus 12:3 NLT - 3 On the eighth day the boy's foreskin must be circumcised.

The new testament says this, on the subject,"

Rachel continues, **"Acts 15:1-21 NLT - 1 While Paul and Barnabas were at Antioch of Syria, some men from Judea arrived and began to teach the believers: 'Unless you are circumcised as required by the law of Moses, you cannot be saved.' 2 Paul and Barnabas disagreed with them, arguing vehemently. Finally, the church decided to send Paul and Barnabas to Jerusalem, accompanied by some local believers, to talk to the apostles and elders about this question. 3 The church sent the delegates to Jerusalem, and they stopped along the way in Phoenicia and Samaria to visit the believers. They told them--much to everyone's joy--that the Gentiles, too, were being converted. 4 When they arrived in Jerusalem, Barnabas and Paul were welcomed by the whole church, including the apostles and elders. They reported everything God had done through them. 5 But then some of the believers who belonged to the sect of the Pharisees stood up and insisted, 'The Gentile converts must be circumcised and required to follow the law of Moses.' 6 So the apostles and elders met together to resolve this issue. 7 At the meeting, after a long discussion, Peter stood and addressed them as follows: 'Brothers, you all know that God chose me from among you some time ago to preach to the Gentiles so**

that they could hear the Good News and believe. 8 God knows people's hearts, and he confirmed that he accepts Gentiles by giving them the Holy Spirit, just as he did to us. 9 He made no distinction between us and them, for he cleansed their hearts through faith. 10 So why are you now challenging God by burdening the Gentile believers with a yoke that neither we nor our ancestors were able to bear? 11 We believe that we are all saved the same way, by the undeserved grace of the Lord Jesus.' 12 Everyone listened quietly as Barnabas and Paul told about the miraculous signs and wonders God had done through them among the Gentiles. 13 When they had finished, James stood and said, 'Brothers, listen to me. 14 Peter has told you about the time God first visited the Gentiles to take from them a people for himself. 15 And this conversion of Gentiles is exactly what the prophets predicted. As it is written: 16 'Afterward I will return and restore the fallen house of David. I will rebuild its ruins and restore it, 17 so that the rest of humanity might seek the LORD, including the Gentiles--all those I have called to be mine. The LORD has spoken-- 18 he who made these things known so long ago.' 19 "And so my judgment is that we should not make it difficult for the Gentiles who are turning to God. 20 Instead, we should write and tell them to abstain from eating food offered to idols, from sexual immorality, from eating the meat of strangled animals, and from consuming blood. 21 For these laws of Moses have been preached in Jewish synagogues in every city on every Sabbath for many generations.'

1 Corinthians 7:17-20 NLT - 17 Each of you should continue to live in whatever situation the Lord has placed you, and remain as you were when God first called you. This is my rule for all the churches. 18 For instance, a man who was circumcised before he became a believer should not try to reverse it. And the man who was uncircumcised when he became a believer should not be circumcised now. 19 For it makes no difference whether or not a man has been circumcised. The important thing is to keep God's commandments. 20 Yes, each of you should remain as you were when God called you.

Galatians 5:6 NLT - 6 For when we place our faith in Christ Jesus, there is no benefit in being circumcised or being uncircumcised. What is important is faith expressing itself in love.

Galatians 6:12-13, 15 NLT - 12 Those who are trying to force you to be circumcised want to look good to others. They don't want to be persecuted for teaching that the cross of Christ alone can save. 13 And even those who advocate circumcision don't keep the whole law themselves. They only want you to be circumcised so they can boast about it and claim you as their disciples. ... 15 It doesn't matter whether we have been circumcised or not. What counts is whether we have been transformed into a new creation." Rachel ends her reading.

"There are other scriptures that say the same thing. Have we covered enough or do you want more?" Martha asks.

"No, I think we get the gist of it," Lisa and Becky say.

Crystal says, "Well, I still think it is good to circumcise baby boys if for no other reason than it is healthier and more sanitary."

Rachel says, "I agree with Crystal, I think God wants us to continue to circumcise our baby boys, but if a grown man is uncircumcised and becomes a Christian then his heart is circumcised and he is not obligated to be circumcised in any other way."

"Well put, I believe that too. Thank you, Crystal and Rachel. What else did you find Rachel?" Martha asks.

"There's **Genesis 1:28**." Rachel reads, **"Genesis 1:28 NLT - 28 Then God blessed them and said, 'Be fruitful and multiply. Fill the earth and govern it. Reign over the fish in the sea, the birds in the sky, and all the animals that scurry along the ground.'**

He also said the same thing to the sons of Noah.

Genesis 9:1 NLT - 1 Then God blessed Noah and his sons and told them, "Be fruitful and multiply. Fill the earth.'"

"I think we have done a good job of doing that," Becky says.

Martha says, "I don't think this was a commandment, as much as a statement. or permission to have lots of children until the world is occupied. Now that the world has been 'filled' I think we need to be responsible. I don't think there is the need to be quite so 'fruitful' anymore. I don't believe it is a sin to not have children. Some people can't have children and some people never get the chance, or simply don't want children."

"I think it is now a personal choice on how many children we bring into the world and not a commandment for all time, lest he would have said so as he did with all of the other commandments," Rachel says.

Crystal says, "I agree with that. One will be plenty for me. Unless it's a boy then I will try one more time for my baby girl."

Becky agrees also, "What else is in Genesis that could be considered a commandment?"

Rachel says, "Well, let's read on and see. **Genesis 9:2-6, 12-13 NLT - 2 All the animals of the earth, all the birds of the sky, all the small animals that scurry along the ground, and all the fish in the sea will look on you with fear and terror. I have placed them in your power. 3 I have given them to you for food, just as I have given you grain and vegetables. 4 But you must never eat any meat that still has the lifeblood in it. 5 "And I will require the blood of anyone who takes another person's life. If a wild animal kills a person, it must die. And anyone who murders a fellow human must die. 6 If anyone takes a human life, that person's life will also be taken by human hands. For God made human beings in his own image. ... 12 Then God said, 'I am giving you a sign of my covenant with you and with all living creatures, for all generations to come. 13 I have placed my rainbow in the clouds. It is the sign of my covenant with you and with all the earth."**

Lisa asks, "We aren't suppose to eat blood? This is the first I've heard of this. Is there more on this subject?"

Martha answers, "Yes, there is. Shall we look up 'blood' and see what the Bible says on the subject?"

"Yes, please," Lisa says.

Crystal looks on and says," Wow there's 261 verses about blood. We aren't going to look up all of them are we?"

Rachel gently states, "No, only the ones pertaining to eating it." She reads, "**Leviticus 3:17 NLT - 17 You must never eat any fat or blood. This is a permanent law for you, and it must be observed from generation to generation, wherever you live.**

Leviticus 17:12, 14 NLT - 12 That is why I have said to the people of Israel, 'You must never eat or drink blood-- neither you nor the foreigners living among you.' ... 14 The life of every creature is in its blood. That is why I have said to the people of Israel, 'You must never eat or drink blood, for the life of any creature is in its blood.' So whoever consumes blood will be cut off from the community.'

Leviticus 19:26 NLT - 26 "Do not eat meat that has not been drained of its blood. Do not practice fortune-telling or witchcraft."

Rachel says, "This is why the bible says not to eat an animal that has been strangled rather than having been slaughtered by having its throat cut and the blood drained out. A strangled animal has all of its blood still in it. And once an animal is dead, it is pretty much impossible to get it all out."

Crystal says, "Yuk, I wouldn't eat it or drink blood anyway. That's gross."

Martha says, "I'm afraid you eat more blood then you think you do."

Rachel adds, "Yeah, What do you think gives meat it's flavor anyway?"

Becky asks, "Is that why you guys are all vegetarians?"

Martha says, "That's part of it yes. The Bible says we are not to eat or drink blood or the fat of an animal. Meat that has been totally eliminated of blood and fat is pretty much tasteless."

"We can't eat fat either? Where does it say that again?" Lisa asks.

"Leviticus 7:23 NLT - 23 Give the following instructions to the people of Israel. You must never eat fat, whether from cattle, sheep, or goats.

Leviticus 3:17 NLT - 17 You must never eat any fat or blood. This is a permanent law for you, and it must be observed from generation to generation, wherever you live." Rachel reads.

All Lisa can say is, "Oh."

"Do you want to continue with what the Bible says we are to eat and not eat?" Martha asks.

Crystal says, "There's more?"

Rachel says "Yes, there's a lot more actually. But first I want to examine **Genesis 9,** God is talking to Noah right after they get off the ark. **Genesis 9:2-3 NLT - 2 All the animals of the earth, all the birds of the sky, all the small animals that scurry along the ground, and all the fish in the sea will look on you with fear and terror. I have placed them in your power. 3 <u>I have given them to you for food</u>, just as I have given you grain and vegetables.** God said all animals are for food. Right? But Noah only took two each of the unclean animals on board one male and one female, if they ate any of them that would have ended their existence right there. He took seven pairs of the clean animals so the people could eat them without fear of causing that animal to become extinct. As long as they left one male and one female alive. Besides there were only like eight people on the earth, one animal would feed all of them for a long time, so they didn't need to kill all of the animals just one once in a while. Let me read. **Genesis 7:2 NLT - 2 Take with you seven pairs--male and female--of each animal I have approved for eating and for sacrifice, and take one pair of each of the others."**

Becky says, "This sounds interesting, I want to know more."

Martha says, "The Bible says in **Leviticus 10:8-10 NLT - 8 Then the LORD said to Aaron, 9 'You and your descendants must never drink wine or any other alcoholic drink before going into the Tabernacle. If you do, you will die. This is a permanent law for you, and it must be observed from generation to generation. 10 You must distinguish between what is sacred and what is common, between what is ceremonially unclean and what is clean.'"**

Crystal asks, "It said 'ceremonially unclean.' You don't keep the ceremonies they did. Do you?"

Rachel says, "First the word 'ceremonially' is added by the translators, and, no,we do not follow the ceremonies of the Pharisees. The Pharisees added a bunch of their own rules God didn't have to begin with. Let's get back to **Leviticus 10:10,** from Young's Literal Translation.

"Leviticus 10:10 YLT - 10 so as to make a separation between the holy and the common, and between the unclean and the pure;

"See the word ceremonial is not there."

"Oh," Crystal says. "well, I don't drink alcohol anyway so that's not a big deal for me. I'm allergic."

"Us either," Becky and Lisa say. Lisa adds, "Baptists don't drink alcohol." Becky adds under her breath, "Not very often anyway. I don't really like alcohol, so I can take it or leave it, and never until I get drunk. Been there, done that, don't care to do it ever again."

Martha says, "That's good. But sometimes it's ok to have a glass of wine. In fact in Jesus' day wine was the main thing they drank. They didn't have the water purification plants that we have today, but they did drink water, it wasn't as polluted as it is today."

Martha reads, "**1 Timothy 5:23 NLT - 23 Don't drink only water. You ought to drink a little wine for the sake of your stomach because you are sick so often.**

I don't think they had coffee. So it was wine or goat's milk or water. But if someone has a problem with alcohol, an allergy, or they are an alcoholic, then they should abstain from all alcohol. In fact the Bible does tell us to stay away from 'hard' liquor, but there is nothing wrong with a glass of wine as long as you don't get drunk. It is wrong to get drunk, then you are numbing your mind and opening yourself up for Satan to come in and control your life. Let me read.

Ephesians 5:18 NLT - 18 Don't be drunk with wine, because that will ruin your life. Instead, be filled with the Holy Spirit,

Isaiah 5:11 NLT - 11 What sorrow for those who get up early in the morning looking for a drink of alcohol and spend long evenings drinking wine to make themselves flaming drunk.

So you can see it is not good to get drunk, but a glass of wine once in a while is ok. Shall we move on?" Martha finishes,

Becky says, "Yes, please."

Martha looks at Rachel and she reads, **"Leviticus 11:1-47 NLT - 1 Then the LORD said to Moses and Aaron, 2 'Give the following instructions to the people of Israel. Of all the land animals, these are the ones you may use for food. 3 You may eat any animal that has completely split hooves and chews the cud. 4 You may not, however, eat the following animals that have split hooves or that chew the cud, but not both. The camel chews the cud but does not have split hooves, so it is unclean for you. 5 The hyrax chews the cud but does not have split hooves, so it is unclean. 6 The hare chews the cud but does not have split hooves, so it is unclean. 7 The pig has evenly split hooves but does not chew the cud, so it is unclean. 8 You may not eat the meat of these animals or even touch their carcasses. They are unclean for you. 9 Of all the marine animals, these are ones you may use for food. You may eat anything from the water if it has both fins and scales, whether taken from salt water or from streams. 10 But you must never eat animals from the sea or from rivers that do not have both fins and scales. They are detestable to you. This applies both to little creatures that live in shallow water and to all creatures that live in deep water. 11 They will always be detestable to you. You must never eat their meat or even touch their dead bodies. 12 Any marine animal that does not have both fins and scales is detestable to you. 13 These are the birds**

**that are detestable to you. You must never eat them: the
griffon vulture, the bearded vulture, the black vulture,
14 the kite, falcons of all kinds, 15 ravens of all kinds, 16
the eagle owl, the short-eared owl, the seagull, hawks of
all kinds, 17 the little owl, the cormorant, the great owl,
18 the barn owl, the desert owl, the Egyptian vulture, 19
the stork, herons of all kinds, the hoopoe, and the bat.
20 You must not eat winged insects that walk along the
ground; they are detestable to you. 21 You may, however,
eat winged insects that walk along the ground and have
jointed legs so they can jump. 22 The insects you are
permitted to eat include all kinds of locusts, bald locusts,
crickets, and grasshoppers. 23 All other winged insects
that walk along the ground are detestable to you. 24 The
following creatures will make you unclean. If any of you
touch their carcasses, you will be defiled until evening. 25
If you pick up their carcasses, you must wash your clothes,
and you will remain defiled until evening. 26 Any animal
that has split hooves that are not evenly divided or that
does not chew the cud is unclean for you. If you touch the
carcass of such an animal, you will be defiled. 27 Of the
animals that walk on all fours, those that have paws are
unclean. If you touch the carcass of such an animal, you
will be defiled until evening. 28 If you pick up its carcass,
you must wash your clothes, and you will remain defiled
until evening. These animals are unclean for you. 29 Of
the small animals that scurry along the ground, these
are unclean for you: the mole rat, the rat, large lizards of
all kinds, 30 the gecko, the monitor lizard, the common
lizard, the sand lizard, and the chameleon. 31 All these**

small animals are unclean for you. If any of you touch the dead body of such an animal, you will be defiled until evening. 32 If such an animal dies and falls on something, that object will be unclean. This is true whether the object is made of wood, cloth, leather, or burlap. Whatever its use, you must dip it in water, and it will remain defiled until evening. After that, it will be clean and may be used again. 33 If such an animal falls into a clay pot, everything in the pot will be defiled, and the pot must be smashed. 34 If the water from such a container spills on any food, the food will be defiled. And any beverage in such a container will be defiled. 35 Any object on which the carcass of such an animal falls will be defiled. If it is an oven or hearth, it must be destroyed, for it is defiled, and you must treat it accordingly. 36 However, if the carcass of such an animal falls into a spring or a cistern, the water will still be clean. But anyone who touches the carcass will be defiled. 37 If the carcass falls on seed grain to be planted in the field, the seed will still be considered clean. 38 But if the seed is wet when the carcass falls on it, the seed will be defiled. 39 If an animal you are permitted to eat dies and you touch its carcass, you will be defiled until evening. 40 If you eat any of its meat or carry away its carcass, you must wash your clothes, and you will remain defiled until evening. 41 All small animals that scurry along the ground are detestable, and you must never eat them. 42 This includes all animals that slither along on their bellies, as well as those with four legs and those with many feet. All such animals that scurry along the ground are detestable, and you must never eat them.

43 Do not defile yourselves by touching them. You must not make yourselves unclean because of them. 44 For I am the LORD your God. You must consecrate yourselves and be holy, because I am holy. So do not defile yourselves with any of these small animals that scurry along the ground. 45 For I, the LORD, am the one who brought you up from the land of Egypt, that I might be your God. Therefore, you must be holy because I am holy. 46 These are the instructions regarding land animals, birds, marine creatures, and animals that scurry along the ground. 47 By these instructions you will know what is unclean and clean, and which animals may be eaten and which may not be eaten.'" Rachel ends her reading**.**

Crystal with her eyes wide open says, "Pigs? That's pork, right?" She jumps up from her chair and starts to pace around as she continues. "I love pork. I can't eat pork? But our old pastor said we didn't have to follow the old testament stuff."

Rachel takes a deep breath and says, "We believe that the old testament complements the new and that the whole Bible is good. Let me read what the new testament says about <u>all</u> Scripture. **2 Timothy 3:16 NKJV - 16 All Scripture** (old and new) **is given by inspiration of God, and is profitable for doctrine, for reproof, for correction, for instruction in righteousness,**

This is talking about the old testament. The new one had not been written yet."

Crystal sits down with a frown on her face and mumbles to herself about how she will eat what she wants.

Becky says, "I never liked pork."

Rachel asks, "Why's that?"

Becky explains. "I had an Uncle who owned a pig farm. I went there when I was little, there was a cute little piglet that I fell in love with, he was so smart and cute and he would follow me around like a puppy. I really loved that pig I named him George. We stayed there for three or four days, anyway on the last day there, my uncle came out and said 'in honor of all of you being here we are going to have a feast tonight.' And then he grabbed George by the hind leg and picked him up and carried the loudly squealing piglet off to a building. I followed and watched him kill George. Then cut him up. At dinner I looked at the meat on the table and asked 'is that the pig you killed earlier today?' and my Uncle said 'yes'. I ran to my room threw myself on the bed and cried and cried. My Mom came in and asked what was wrong and I told her 'that was George, he was my friend. I will never eat George.' She tried to tell me how the farm was a business and pigs were raised for food, not pets. But I wouldn't have it. And refused to come back until morning. I could hear my Uncle getting mad and yelling something about how he would make me come down and eat the pork. When Mom said 'let her be'. He went out the door and slammed it behind him, still complaining. We never went back, and I never ate anything pork after that. If I know it was pork, I didn't eat it. Mom and Dad tried to get me to eat bacon or pepperoni, but I wouldn't. When Mom bought pork I would go into such a rant on how smart pigs were and how mean it was to kill them, then I would refuse to go anywhere near the offensive meat. Mom actually stopped buying pork all together. To this day I refuse to eat pork. And now I know that eating pork goes against Gods commandments. I'm definitely not eating pork, or any other meat for that matter. I think it's wrong to kill innocent animals just to satisfy our perverted appetites."

Crystal starts to argue about how the animals are put here for our benefit. But Martha gently stops her by saying "To each their own. Becky has her feelings and beliefs and you have yours. Neither one of you is going to change the mind of the other one, so it is pointless to argue about it. Besides Becky didn't make the rules, God did."

Rachel says; "If someone is convinced that Pigs are now clean, then I have a Question."

This gets Crystals attention, and she sits up a little straighter.

Rachel continues, "If pigs are clean and good for food, then aren't all animals clean and ok to eat? So I ask, if you eat pork then would you eat a horse or a dog? Or a rodent? Is there anything that totally grosses you out at the thought of eating it? So much so, that you would never eat it? Why? Why do you think it's wrong to eat a mouse but not a pig? The Bible lumps eating pork, rodents, and other unclean things all in the same category."

She reads, "**Isaiah 66:17 NKJV - 17 ….Those who go to the gardens After an idol in the midst, Eating swine's flesh and the abomination and the mouse, Shall be consumed together," says the LORD.**

This is commonly believed to be talking about the end times. Not old testament times. Of course, I'm sure you can tell me all kinds of reasons why you would eat a pig and not a mouse or even another human being. But truly, if you think about it there really isn't any difference, unclean to God is still unclean." Rachel says.

Crystals says, still a bit pouty, "I'll have to think about that. I still like pork, but the thought of eating mice! That's gross. And cannibalism is illegal, I'm sure."

Lisa says, "I watched a video once that showed someone cooking a fresh piece of pork, and these gross worms started coming out of the meat. I decided then that pork wasn't good."

Crystal makes a face that says, "*Yeah, sure, I'll believe that when I see it.*"

Lisa says, "I found it on You Tube. If you really want to, you can watch it there. Just look up 'cooking pork'."

At this time someone sticks their head in the door and says, "Times up". The group goes out to the main room for lunch.

Lisa says, "Lunch, really, who can eat after that Bible study?"

Becky leans into her friend as they walk out, and says, "It's ok, it's all vegetarian here. No meat, gross or not."

Crystal avoids Becky and Lisa. When the men came out of their room, Jeff, Crystal's husband, is just as excited as Lisa and Becky are about learning about Gods commandments. Which makes Crystal even more unhappy. The sermon is on judgment. The following scriptures are sited,

"Romans 14: 1 Welcome with open arms fellow believers who don't see things the way you do. And don't jump all over them every time they do or say something you don't agree with - even when it seems that they are strong on opinions but weak in the faith department.

Remember, they have their own history to deal with. Treat them gently.

"Isaiah 11:3 NLT - 3 He will delight in obeying the LORD. He will not judge by appearance nor make a decision based on hearsay.

"Luke 6:37 NLT - 37 Do not judge others, and you will not be judged. Do not condemn others, or it will all come back against you. Forgive others, and you will be forgiven.

"John 3:17 NLT - 17 God sent his Son into the world not to judge the world, but to save the world through him.

"James 4:11 NLT - 11 Don't speak evil against each other, dear brothers and sisters. If you criticize and judge each other, then you are criticizing and judging God's law. But your job is to obey the law, not to judge whether it applies to you.

"Romans 14:6 NLT - 6 Those who worship the Lord on a special day do it to honor him. Those who eat any kind of food do so to honor the Lord, since they give thanks to God before eating. And those who refuse to eat certain foods also want to please the Lord and give thanks to God.

"Colossians 2:16-17 NKJV - 16 So let no one judge you in food or in drink, or regarding a festival or a new moon or Sabbaths, 17 which are a shadow of things to come, but the substance is of Christ."

Tom states, "The main theme of this scripture is LET NO ONE JUDGE YOU. And equally important is, we are not to judge others either."

When Crystal hears this she turns and looks at Becky, and almost sticks her tongue out at her. She doesn't, but does give her a very evil look.

Becky thinks Crystal is being childish, but takes the sermon to heart and tries not to judge Crystal.

Becky tries to talk to Crystal but Martha tells her, "Leave her alone for now she may come around, but if she doesn't, it's OK, not everyone is called to be God's chosen people. She will come around one day. And remember **Romans 14**."

So Becky leaves her alone. She also decides to read all of Romans 14 when she gets a chance. The rest of the Sabbath goes by without any further problems. Now it is time to go home. Becky, Lisa and Elisa decide to walk home and enjoy the nice weather. At least, that's what they tell Jeff. Though that is part of it, really they didn't want to endure the stress they know Crystal would inflict on them by her silence and her stares in the car.

Elisa is very excited about her new friend Samantha and tells the two ladies all about her, all the way home. This is good because it takes the women's minds off of Crystal. Lisa does manage to ask Becky, "Where did you dig her up from?" But Becky only has time to shrug her shoulders.

Lisa also comments, "Oh well, that's probably the last time she will show up to church anyway."

Becky thinks, "I don't know her husband seems to be really into it all." But she doesn't get a chance to say anything. The women don't want to discourage Elisa by silencing her, and Becky really doesn't want to talk about it anyway. She has a lot to think about. Especially after the sermon about not judging people. "It is God's place to judge, not ours,"

Tom had said. So instead of judging Crystal, Becky prays for Crystal.

Becky finds it hard to go to sleep that night. Every time she thinks of Crystal, her mind wants to dwell on revenge, but she knows that is wrong, and forces herself to remember what Tom said the night before, and she prays for forgiveness, for both herself and for Crystal, and that God will change Crystal's mind.

-7-

Becky gets up late Sunday morning. The strife with Crystal is almost forgotten as she goes about straightening up her apartment and getting ready to vacuum. After that she is going to have to do her laundry. "*Ugh, that means lugging everything down to the shared laundry room and back again. And what if I run into Crystal there? Maybe I should just pack it all up and go to a different laundromat.*" As she is trying to decide what to do, there is a knock on her door. Becky wonders who that could be. She looks out the peep hole and is surprised to see Crystal standing there. She hopes she isn't there to pick a fight. She even thinks about pretending not to be home, but she opens the door and invites Crystal in. Becky offers Crystal something to drink, but Crystal turns it down.

Crystal starts by humbly saying, "Becky, I'm sorry, I know it's not your fault that the Bible says what it says. I was upset about having to give up pork, especially bacon. I really love bacon. But it was wrong of me to take it out on you and Lisa. I don't even know Lisa. I don't really know you either, but I would like to get know you. So please forgive me." Crystal looks at Becky with tears beginning to show in her eyes.

Becky is pleasantly surprised by this and hugs Crystal out of impulse, and says, "Of course, I forgive you, I prayed for this to happen, and now here you are. I would love to get to know you better too."

Crystal brightens up instantly and hugs Becky back. "I was so afraid you would hold it against me, the way I acted. Thank you so much for forgiving me."

"So, can you stay for a bit? I'm afraid the place is a bit messy, but if you can overlook the dirt I would love it if you can stay and we can talk for a while?" Becky asks.

Crystal looks around and says, "The place looks great. I wish my apartment looked this good. How did you manage to get a two bedroom? We could only get a one bedroom, but we really need a two bedroom. Jeff has a lot of stuff. And with the baby coming and all…. But we'll get by."

Becky says, "I wish I had a one bedroom. I don't need all of this room, or the extra expense. I use to have a roommate but she left recently. And now I have to pay for everything on my own. I was told there weren't any apartments left of any size. So I guess I'm stuck with this one until someone moves out."

"Yes, us too." Crystal sighs.

They sit quiet for a second or two when Becky remembers her manners and says, "Would you like that drink now? I can offer you some water or a root beer."

"Ok, water is fine," Crystal says.

Becky goes to the kitchen and gets two glasses, puts some ice in them, and fills them both with water from her filtered pitcher that she keeps in the refrigerator. She then takes the water back to the living room and sits down in the chair next to the couch, where Crystal is sitting.

"So, tell me, what made you change your mind about being mad at me?" Becky asks.

"It was my wonderful husband, he pointed out that it wasn't your fault the Bible said what it said. And after thinking about it, I realized he was right. Besides I think you were just as surprised about what you learned as I was. You just excepted it faster, that's all," Crystal confesses.

Becky states, "Yes, this is all very new to me too. I only became a Christian a couple of months ago."

Crystal says, "Oh, wow, I didn't realize that."

Again there is a pause in the conversation.

Then Crystal enthusiastically says, "Guess what I found at the grocery store?"

Becky looks at her and asks, "What did you find?" equally enthused and impressed that she had time to go to the store already. She has barely gotten out of bed herself.

"Turkey bacon, and all beef bacon. They even have fake bacon, I mean vegetarian bacon. I bought it all to see which one I might like. Cooked up some of each this morning. I think I like the turkey bacon best. Then believe it or not the second best is the veggie stuff. But the beef bacon is alright too," Crystal says.

Becky says, "Wow, I can't believe you've been up long enough to go to the store and cook breakfast."

Crystal laughs, "No, silly we went to the store last night. Jeff has to get up early to go to work, so I get up and fix him a good breakfast every morning. Besides we only have one car, so when Jeff goes to work I'm left without a car to go anywhere."

"Oh," Becky says, "Sorry you don't have a car of your own, but it's impressive that you get up and cook breakfast every morning for your husband. Not too many women would do that, not if they didn't have to. My breakfast, when I eat breakfast, is usually a bowl of cold cereal."

Crystal is shocked and says, "You're kidding, breakfast is the most important meal of the day. And my biggest meal of the day. So I guess you haven't had breakfast yet?"

Becky confesses, "No, not yet."

Crystal grabs Becky by the hand and says, "You are coming with me, I'm going to fix you a terrific breakfast. I love to cook. My Mother is a nutritionist and my dad is a professional chef. I learned to cook from my dad and what to cook from my mom."

Crystal barely allows Becky to lock her door as she half drags the shocked and giggling Becky to her own apartment just a few doors down. Becky, who is still in her slippers and sweat pants, can't believe she is letting this unusual lady drag her off like this.

"Really, Crystal, this is so sudden, but honestly you don't have to do this you know," Becky says, half protesting, but she really wants to hang out with Crystal. So her protests are more kidding around than not, as Becky pretends to try to leave.

Crystal says, "Oh no, you don't. You're getting a good breakfast if I have to hog tie you down."

At that both girls start to laugh. The banter goes on while Crystal goes into her small kitchen and starts pulling out pots and pans and food. She seems to know what she is doing, so Becky sits on the other side of the breakfast bar and watches in awe. Becky notices that the apartment is cluttered but clean. In no time Crystal is serving up veggie bacon and homemade pancakes with honey or maple syrup . Crystal comes around and sits down next to Becky.

"I remembered you are a vegetarian, so I made you the veggie bacon. I'm having the turkey bacon. I ate with Jeff earlier but I didn't want you to feel left out, so I'll eat a little with you too," Crystal says.

Just then Becky's cell phone rings. She just had time to grab it as Crystal was pulling her out the door.

"Hello," Becky answers. "Oh, Hi Lisa.... What am I doing right now? Well you're not going to believe this but I'm having breakfast with Crystal.....Yes.....Ok,... sounds fun, I'll ask her. See you in an hour then.... Ok, goodbye."

"Was that Lisa from church?" Crystal asks.

"Yes," Becky answers.

"Oh, I wish I could have talked to her. I need to apologize to her too. What did she want? If you don't mind me asking?" Crystal inquires.

"Oh no, that's fine." Becky states. "She wants to go see a movie. It starts in a couple of hours. She invited you to come along, if you would like to."

Crystal perks up, "What are you going to go see?" she asks.

"That new SiFi romance that just came out. I forget the name. Lisa's husband and daughter are going to go see his mother. So Lisa has some time for herself," Becky explains.

"Oh, I know which one you're talking about. I've been wanting to see that movie. But Jeff never wants to go. I'd love to go. Let me put these dishes in the dishwasher, and I'll be ready to go. How was it? Breakfast, I mean?" Crystal asks.

"Fantastic," Becky says, "you're going to spoil me. But I need to go back home and get ready. I don't want to be running around in my grubby clothes and slippers all day."

"Ah, why not? If I looked as good as you, I wouldn't care what I wore, because you look good in anything," Crystal says earnestly.

"Me? are you kidding? You look like a super model. I wish I looked half as good as you," Becky counters. Both girls giggle at the mutual admiration. Then Becky says, "Really, I have to go change. Meet me outside in thirty minutes, Ok?"

"Ok," Crystal says.

The three women meet up in the parking lot. All are wearing casual clothes and flats. Lisa drives them to the mall where the movie is playing. They all talk and laugh and have a good time. After the movie, which they all loved, they do some window shopping, and have lunch at a neighborhood café. Then Lisa drives them home. Becky and Crystal say goodbye and each heads off to their own apartment.

-8-

Lunch on Monday, Lisa and Becky get together to eat.

Lisa starts, "Can you believe the difference in Crystal from Saturday to Sunday? What was that all about?"

Becky says, "I don't know. I think her husband had a lot to do with it. He really seems to be getting into everything the church believes. And Crystal and Jeff really seem to love each other."

Lisa adds, " And remember, Crystal is pregnant. That can really mess with your hormones, especially in the beginning. When I was pregnant with Elisa I was all over the place, as far as my moods went. One second I was laughing, the next crying my eyes out."

"Wow, kind of glad I didn't know you then," Becky kids Lisa. "It's amazing I prayed for Crystal and the very next morning she is at my door saying how sorry she is. That was a fast answer to prayer."

"True, I confess, I prayed for her too. I'm glad it all worked out so well. I guess we will see her at church again after all," Lisa states.

"Yeah, I'm glad about that." Becky changes the subject and asks, "What do you think we will learn about next Sabbath?"

"I don't have a clue," Lisa says.

The banter changes from subject to subject. And soon lunch is over and the women are back at work.

No one is able to get away for a Wednesday meeting, which disappoints Becky, but she hasn't been to the gym in a while and doesn't want to miss too many days, so she goes to the gym on Wednesday instead.

-9-

The week goes by and finally it is Sabbath again. Becky finds herself looking forward to Sabbath. She loves her new friends and it's always a pleasant surprise to find out what new thing they are going to learn about in Sabbath school. The same five women get together for class, after they share breakfast. Crystal is back to her old bubbly self and helps with breakfast. She really seems to be in her element cooking for everyone.

Martha opens with prayer, then asks, "Are there any questions anyone wants answered?"

Crystal answers with, "I have a lot of questions about life and marriage and pregnancy, but nothing about the Bible. I'm almost afraid to find out what new thing I'm going to learn that is going to rock my world and what I thought the Bible and religion was all about."

Martha laughs and says, "Yes, it is surprising to learn what the Bible really says, compared to what the mainstream Christians believe. First to learn that the whole Bible is relevant for today, that the old testament hasn't been done away with. Jesus didn't come to do away with the old, he came to enhance the old, to show the spirit of the old, not just the letter of it."

Rachel adds, "Jesus really didn't bring a new message. it was always there. It was just hidden from them. They were so wrapped up in the do's and don'ts they missed the whole point of it all. And that is love. To love God first foremost, and to love each other, to take care of each other, not to oppress one another. The whole point of the Bible is love and faith, and how to live a long, healthy, and happy life."

"Imagine what life would have been like if Adam and Eve had not sinned," Lisa says. "We would still be in the garden, and we would know Adam and Eve and all the other great people of the Bible."

Crystal says, "I don't know, knowing human nature as I do, I think we would have messed things up sooner or later, and we would still be where we are today."

Martha says, "I believe you are right about that, Miss Crystal. There is just something about human nature that goes against God and all he stands for and all he is."

Becky says, "This is all interesting but I'm ready to get into what the Bible says. What new thing are we going to learn about today. Or should I say old thing that is new to me.

Martha continues, "If you remember when we covered the Sabbath, we talked about a force or power that would think to 'change the times and the seasons'. I want to state right now that the Catholic church of today, didn't change anything. These changes were made a long time ago by someone pretending to be a Christian. From then on Sunday keepers are simply deceived. I don't think God will hold them accountable, unless they refuse to change when the time comes and they are shown the truth. I believe we are all deceived about something. I believe God holds the ones who taught the people to do wrong, responsible. For they knew what was right, but taught, and still teach, the people to do wrong anyway. Maybe they feel trapped into the wrong belief and feel if they tried to correct a centuries old misconception that the people would rebel and kick them out. I don't know. That's for God to Judge. I want all of us to remember that it was the Catholic Church that kept the Bible safe throughout the generations. Without them we wouldn't have this book," she holds up a bible, "to begin with. We must remember it's not our job to criticize and condemn other people and what they believe. If a person believes in God the Father and his Son, Jesus the Christ as their savior, that is what's important for salvation. The rest, though important, is to be left between God and that person. Everyone must 'work out their own salvation' according to how God leads them. As long as they are on the right path, or ladder, to God. It's not our job to judge them but we should guide them when they ask for help. We are here to show people what the Bible says and let them make up their own minds as to what they do with that knowledge. Every Denomination that is a part of Gods church has their part of truth, and should be respected for that. Remember it's not where you are on the path as long as you are on the path. God reveals to each person what they can handle, when they can handle it. So let's proceed with love, not condemnation, and learn for ourselves what the Bible says is right for us."

Rachel says, "Wow, ok then, keeping that in mind, let's see what else was changed as far as 'the times' are concerned." She reads,

"Exodus 12:1-2 NLT - 1 While the Israelites were still in the land of Egypt, the LORD gave the following instructions to Moses and Aaron: 2 'From now on, this month will be the first month of the year for you.'"

Martha asks, "How do we know when this month is? Lets read, **"Leviticus 23. 5 The LORD's Passover begins at sundown on the fourteenth day of the first month."**

When is Passover?" Martha asks.

Lisa says, "Passover, that's when Jesus was crucified, when we celebrate Easter."

Becky says, "Oh, I'm glad we are covering this. Tom mentioned it the other day and I've been waiting for it to come up."

Martha says, "Yes, Lisa, you are right Passover is in the spring. And I'm glad we are learning something you are interested in Becky. Let's see what the Bible says." She reads, **"Leviticus 23:1-44 NLT - 1 The LORD said to Moses, 2 'Give the following instructions to the people of Israel. These are the LORD's appointed festivals, which you are to proclaim as official days for holy assembly. 3 You have six days each week for your ordinary work, but the seventh day is a Sabbath day of complete rest, an official day for holy assembly. It is the LORD's Sabbath day, and it must be observed wherever you live. 4 In addition to the Sabbath, these are the LORD's appointed festivals, the official days for holy assembly that are to be celebrated at their proper times each year. 5 The LORD's Passover begins at sundown on the fourteenth day of the first month. 6 On the next day, the fifteenth day of the month, you must begin celebrating the Festival of Unleavened**

Bread. This festival to the LORD continues for seven days, and during that time the bread you eat must be made without yeast. 7 On the first day of the festival, all the people must stop their ordinary work and observe an official day for holy assembly. 8 For seven days you must present special gifts to the LORD. On the seventh day the people must again stop all their ordinary work to observe an official day for holy assembly.'"

Martha continues, "So the Bible says there are seven Holy Days in addition to the weekly Sabbath. The first one is Passover. What happened to Jesus on Passover? What did he say and do at that time? And what are we to do? Let's find out, **John 13:1-15 NLT - 1 Before the Passover celebration, Jesus knew that his hour had come to leave this world and return to his Father. He had loved his disciples during his ministry on earth, and now he loved them to the very end. 2 It was time for supper, and the devil had already prompted Judas, son of Simon Iscariot, to betray Jesus. 3 Jesus knew that the Father had given him authority over everything and that he had come from God and would return to God. 4 So he got up from the table, took off his robe, wrapped a towel around his waist, 5 and poured water into a basin. Then he began to wash the disciples' feet, drying them with the towel he had around him. 6 When Jesus came to Simon Peter, Peter said to him, 'Lord, are you going to wash my feet?' 7 Jesus replied, 'You don't understand now what I am doing, but someday you will.' 8 'No,' Peter protested, 'you will never ever wash my feet!' Jesus replied, 'Unless I wash you, you won't belong to me.' 9 Simon Peter exclaimed, 'Then wash my hands and head**

as well, Lord, not just my feet!' 10 Jesus replied, 'A person who has bathed all over does not need to wash, except for the feet, to be entirely clean. And you disciples are clean, but not all of you.' 11 For Jesus knew who would betray him. That is what he meant when he said, 'Not all of you are clean.' 12 After washing their feet, he put on his robe again and sat down and asked, 'Do you understand what I was doing? 13 You call me Teacher and Lord, and you are right, because that's what I am. <u>14 And since I, your Lord and Teacher, have washed your feet, you ought to wash each other's feet. 15 I have given you an example to follow. Do as I have done to you.</u>

John 14:15 NLT - 15 'If you love me, obey my commandments.'

Luke 22:15, 19-20 NLT - 15 Jesus said, 'I have been very eager to eat this Passover meal with you before my suffering begins.' ... 19 He took some bread and gave thanks to God for it. Then he broke it in pieces and gave it to the disciples, saying, 'This is my body, which is given for you. Do this to remember me.' 20 After supper he took another cup of wine and said, 'This cup is the new covenant between God and his people--an agreement confirmed with my blood, which is poured out as a sacrifice for you.'

1 Corinthians 11:25 NLT - 25 In the same way, he took the cup of wine after supper, saying, 'This cup is the new covenant between God and his people--an agreement confirmed with my blood. Do this to remember me as often as you drink it.'"

Crystal says, "That's communion. My old church did that every Sunday. Except for the foot washing thing. That sounds gross."

Martha says, "I believe all of the Christian churches do a bread and wine ceremony. Some call it 'Communion', some call it 'the sacrament'. Some do it every Sunday, some every quarter. Some use wine, some use grape juice, some use water. We do it once a year and call it 'the Lord's Supper'. We drink real wine just as Jesus did, but I understand why others would use a non-alcohol version. And, yes, we wash each other's feet. It's not gross, not really, but it is humbling. I find it strange that only some Sabbath keeping churches honor Jesus by doing the Lord's Supper the day before the Jews celebrate their 'Seder' or Passover supper, and most neglect to do the foot washing part, for whatever reason they want to invent, but Jesus said for us to wash each other's feet, so that is what we do. Most Sunday keeping churches wouldn't be caught dead doing a Lord's Supper, or Communion, when Jesus actually did it at Passover. No, they would rather play games and overload on sugar for the day of first fruits, but more on that in a minute.

"Our Lord's Supper and the following week goes like this. Mind you this is just how we do it. It doesn't mean it is the right way or the only way of 'remembering Christ'. It's just how we believe we should do it. I don't believe it is right or wrong to have Communion more often. That is between you and God. This is just how we do it.

First, we meet here at sundown the night before the biblical Passover, because that's when Jesus had his last supper with his disciples. We read from the gospels, each taking their turn reading. Then we separate, the single men and women go to different rooms and the married couples go to another room. Married people can go together or separate, that's their choice, we don't judge. Anyway, we wash each other's feet and when everyone is done, we come back together and then read more scriptures and take the wine and the unleavened bread, all of this in remembrance of Him. Then we sing a song, and read more scriptures about his trial and sentencing, through to his death and burial. Then we go home. It is all very somber. A lot of the women wear black as if they are going to a funeral of a brother or a spouse. The next day we make sure all leavening has been removed from our houses. We usually start using and reducing any leavening for a couple of weeks before. Anyway, we clean out any leftover leaving, like the Bible says we are to do. At sundown we get together again for a Seder service with bitter herbs and unleavened bread and read scriptures about the first Passover. We used to each have a Seder at home, but when we realized everyone wanted to do that, and since some of us are single, we started getting together for a group Seder. Then we actually learned that it was biblical to meet together for a group Seder. Then we go home. The day after the Seder is a Holy Day. Passover Sabbath can happen any day of the week. It actually changes from year to year just as the secular holidays change from year to year. We don't go to work on that Holy Day. We all get together for a sacred assembly. We only eat unleavened bread for the whole seven days of Passover, but only the first and last day are Holy. There is always a Weekly Sabbath in there somewhere. That is when we read about Jesus' resurrection and what he did and said until his ascension into Heaven.

There's no chocolate bunnies or Easter egg hunts or any of the other pagan trappings that have nothing to do with Jesus or his resurrection. On the last day of Passover we have another Holy Day that begins and ends at sundown. Then it's to the store after sundown for bread again. That's not required of course, it just works out that way, the buying of leavened bread after sundown, I mean. We don't take the whole week off from work, but I've been told that some Churches of God do. Neither is right or wrong, that again is an individual decision."

Becky, Lisa, and Crystal all stare at Martha. Lisa finally says, "Wow, that is so different from what we are used too."

Becky says, "Wait, Easter is pagan? What's a pagan?"

Lisa says, "They believe in a multitude of gods, and in the old days used to sacrifice children to their gods. And they had orgies, and worshiped sex and sex goddesses, and death, and all sorts of evil things. I don't know what they do now, but I do know paganism is alive and well and has many followers today."

Crystal says, "Gross."

Martha says, "You are right, Lisa. How did you know?"

"My husband's brother's ex-wife is a pagan, so I looked it up, to see what she believes or at least what the pagans did in biblical days. It was a real eye opener. Like I said, I don't know what their 'worship' service is like today, I could ask her if I really wanted to know, but I don't really want to know, since the Bible says not to inquire about such things," Lisa says.

Crystal says, "Oh, I'm sorry to hear that there still are pagans today and that an ex-family member of yours is one. So how is Easter pagan?"

Rachel pipes in and says, "The word 'Easter' was not originally found in the Bible. The King James version mistranslates Passover as Easter one time.

Acts 12:4 KJV - 4 And when he had apprehended him, he put him in prison, and delivered him to four quaternion's of soldiers to keep him; intending after *Easter* to bring him forth to the people.

But Young's Literal Translation says.

Acts 12:4 YLT - 4 whom also having seized, he did put in prison, having delivered him to four quaternion's of soldiers to guard him, intending after the Passover to bring him forth to the people. So as you can see, the word should be Passover not Easter. Who knows why they translated it that way." Rachel says.

Martha adds. "What does chocolate bunnies and eggs have to do with Jesus anyway?"

Rachel continues, "Easter is probably a miss pronunciation of the pagan goddess Ishtar. Which was the goddess of sex, if I remember correctly."

"Oh," Crystal says sounding disappointed. "Why do I get the feeling Christmas is out too?"

Rachel says, "You guessed it. But we are getting ahead of ourselves."

Martha continues, "The first day of the week, or Sunday, or the day after the Weekly Sabbath that falls in during the days of unleavened bread, is called first fruits. A day when the priests would waive a shaft of the newly harvested grain in front of God. It is also proclaimed to be the day Jesus rose from the grave to be the first fruits of the resurrected Christian brethren, when Jesus comes again. This is, as far as we can tell, not a Holly Day. And since none of us are farmers, we don't have a first harvest to bring to the Lord. Lets read it, **Leviticus 23: 9 Then the LORD said to Moses, 10 'Give the following instructions to the people of Israel. When you enter the land I am giving you and you harvest its first crops, bring the priest a bundle of grain from the first cutting of your grain harvest. 11 On the day after the Sabbath, the priest will lift it up before the LORD so it may be accepted on your behalf. 12 On that same day you must sacrifice a one-year-old male lamb with no defects as a burnt offering to the LORD. 13 With it you must present a grain offering consisting of four quarts of choice flour moistened with olive oil. It will be a special gift, a pleasing aroma to the LORD. You must also offer one quart of wine as a liquid offering. 14 Do not eat any bread or roasted grain or fresh kernels on that day until you bring this offering to your God. This is a permanent law for you, and it must be observed from generation to generation wherever you live.'"**

"Sounds like a poor excuse to me, for not doing something God said to do," Crystal mumbles.

Martha says, "You know, you are right. I think we should look into acknowledging the day. Bring a special offering of food to the poor on that day. Thank you, Crystal, that's an excellent idea."

Crystal brightens up and smiles, kind of proud of herself for coming up with something new that came from the Bible..

Rachel says, "The next Holy Day is Pentecost. It happens late spring. Let me read it, **Leviticus 23:15 From the day after the Sabbath--the day you bring the bundle of grain**

to be lifted up as a special offering--count off seven full weeks. 16. Keep counting until the day after the seventh Sabbath, fifty days later. Then present an offering of new grain to the LORD. 17 From wherever you live, bring two loaves of bread to be lifted up before the LORD as a special offering. Make these loaves from four quarts of choice flour, and bake them with yeast. They will be an offering to the LORD from the first of your crops. 18 Along with the bread, present seven one-year-old male lambs with no defects, one young bull, and two rams as burnt offerings to the LORD. These burnt offerings, together with the grain offerings and liquid offerings, will be a special gift, a pleasing aroma to the LORD. 19 Then you must offer one male goat as a sin offering and two one-year-old male lambs as a peace offering. 20 The priest will lift up the two lambs as a special offering to the LORD, together with the loaves representing the first of your crops. These offerings, which are holy to the LORD, belong to the priests. 21 That same day will be proclaimed an official day for holy assembly, a day on which you do no ordinary work. This is a permanent law for you, and it must be observed from generation to generation wherever you live. 22 When you harvest the crops of your land, do not harvest the grain along the edges of your fields, and do not pick up what the harvesters drop. Leave it for the poor and the foreigners living among you. I am the LORD your God."

Martha says, "Remember we read how Jesus was our ultimate, and therefore, our final need for sacrifice? So we don't make animal sacrifices anymore, and we don't have the

Levites around to give bread to either. But I think it would be good to give food to a food bank on that day. Anyway the fiftieth day or Pentecost which means fifty or fiftieth, is a Holy Day. So what happened on Pentecost after Jesus went back to heaven?" Martha asks, then reads, **"Acts 2:1-9, 11-16 NLT -
1 On the day of Pentecost all the believers were meeting together in one place. 2 Suddenly, there was a sound from heaven like the roaring of a mighty windstorm, and it filled the house where they were sitting. 3 Then, what looked like flames or tongues of fire appeared and settled on each of them. 4 And everyone present was filled with the Holy Spirit and began speaking in other languages, as the Holy Spirit gave them this ability. 5 At that time there were devout Jews from every nation living in Jerusalem. 6
When they heard the loud noise, everyone came running, and they were bewildered to hear their own languages being spoken by the believers. 7 They were completely amazed. 'How can this be?' they exclaimed. 'These people are all from Galilee, 8 and yet we hear them speaking in our own native languages! 9 Here we are--Parthians, Medes, Elamites, people from Mesopotamia, Judea, Cappadocia, Pontus, the province of Asia, ... 11 (both Jews and converts to Judaism), Cretans, and Arabs. And we all hear these people speaking in our own languages about the wonderful things God has done!' 12 They stood there amazed and perplexed. 'What can this mean?' they asked each other. 13 But others in the crowd ridiculed them, saying, 'They're just drunk, that's all!' 14 Then Peter stepped forward with the eleven other apostles and shouted to the crowd, 'Listen carefully, all of you, fellow**

Jews and residents of Jerusalem! Make no mistake about this. 15 These people are not drunk, as some of you are assuming. Nine o'clock in the morning is much too early for that. 16 No, what you see was predicted long ago by the prophet Joel.'"

Crystal says, "I went to a Pentecostal church once. It was weird, kind-a scary actually. Everyone was pretending to talk in some unknown language, everyone at once. It was very chaotic. Do you do that on Pentecost?"

Martha smiles and says, "No, I suggest we see what the Bible says about speaking in tongues."

Rachel says, "I've got the scriptures here." And she reads, **"1 Corinthians 14:1-40 NLT - 1 Let love be your highest goal! But you should also desire the special abilities the Spirit gives--especially the ability to prophesy. 2 For if you have the ability to speak in tongues, you will be talking only to God, since people won't be able to understand you. You will be speaking by the power of the Spirit, but it will all be mysterious. 3 But one who prophesies strengthens others, encourages them, and comforts them. 4 A person who speaks in tongues is strengthened personally, but one who speaks a word of prophecy strengthens the entire church. 5 I wish you could all speak in tongues, but even more I wish you could all prophesy. For prophecy is greater than speaking in tongues, unless someone interprets what you are saying so that the whole church will be strengthened. 6 Dear brothers and sisters, if I should come to you speaking in an unknown language, how would that help you? But if I bring you a revelation or some special knowledge or prophecy or teaching, that**

will be helpful. 7 Even lifeless instruments like the flute or the harp must play the notes clearly, or no one will recognize the melody. 8 And if the bugler doesn't sound a clear call, how will the soldiers know they are being called to battle? 9 It's the same for you. If you speak to people in words they don't understand, how will they know what you are saying? You might as well be talking into empty space. 10 There are many different languages in the world, and every language has meaning. 11 But if I don't understand a language, I will be a foreigner to someone who speaks it, and the one who speaks it will be a foreigner to me. 12 And the same is true for you. Since you are so eager to have the special abilities the Spirit gives, seek those that will strengthen the whole church. 13 So anyone who speaks in tongues should pray also for the ability to interpret what has been said. 14 For if I pray in tongues, my spirit is praying, but I don't understand what I am saying. 15 Well then, what shall I do? I will pray in the spirit, and I will also pray in words I understand. I will sing in the spirit, and I will also sing in words I understand. 16 For if you praise God only in the spirit, how can those who don't understand you praise God along with you? How can they join you in giving thanks when they don't understand what you are saying? 17 You will be giving thanks very well, but it won't strengthen the people who hear you. 18 I thank God that I speak in tongues more than any of you. 19 But in a church meeting I would rather speak five understandable words to help others than ten thousand words in an unknown language. 20 Dear brothers and sisters, don't be childish in your

understanding of these things. Be innocent as babies when it comes to evil, but be mature in understanding matters of this kind. 21 It is written in the Scriptures: 'I will speak to my own people through strange languages and through the lips of foreigners. But even then, they will not listen to me,' says the LORD. 22 So you see that speaking in tongues is a sign, not for believers, but for unbelievers. Prophecy, however, is for the benefit of believers, not unbelievers. 23 Even so, if unbelievers or people who don't understand these things come into your church meeting and hear everyone speaking in an unknown language, they will think you are crazy. 24 But if all of you are prophesying, and unbelievers or people who don't understand these things come into your meeting, they will be convicted of sin and judged by what you say. 25 As they listen, their secret thoughts will be exposed, and they will fall to their knees and worship God, declaring, 'God is truly here among you.' 26 Well, my brothers and sisters, let's summarize. When you meet together, one will sing, another will teach, another will tell some special revelation God has given, one will speak in tongues, and another will interpret what is said. But everything that is done must strengthen all of you. 27 No more than two or three should speak in tongues. They must speak one at a time, and someone must interpret what they say. 28 But if no one is present who can interpret, they must be silent in your church meeting and speak in tongues to God privately. 29 Let two or three people prophesy, and let the others evaluate what is said. 30 But if someone is prophesying and another person receives a revelation

**from the Lord, the one who is speaking must stop. 31
In this way, all who prophesy will have a turn to speak,
one after the other, so that everyone will learn and be
encouraged. 32 Remember that people who prophesy are
in control of their spirit and can take turns. 33 For God is
not a God of disorder but of peace, as in all the meetings
of God's holy people. 34 Women should be silent during
the church meetings. It is not proper for them to speak.
They should be submissive, just as the law says. 35 If
they have any questions, they should ask their husbands
at home, for it is improper for women to speak in church
meetings. 36 Or do you think God's word originated with
you Corinthians? Are you the only ones to whom it was
given? 37 If you claim to be a prophet or think you are
spiritual, you should recognize that what I am saying is
a command from the Lord himself. 38 But if you do not
recognize this, you yourself will not be recognized. 39
So, my dear brothers and sisters, be eager to prophesy,
and don't forbid speaking in tongues. 40 But be sure that
everything is done properly and in order."**

"Thank you, Rachel, I do not know if people in Pentecostal churches are 'faking it' or not. But they should follow what 1Corinthians 14 says and only do it when there is an interpreter and only one at a time**. 1 Corinthians 14:33 NLT - 33 For God is not a God of disorder but of peace, as in all the meetings of God's holy people. For God is a God of order and not disorder,"** Martha says.

Crystal states, "Well, I know it isn't for me."

Rachel says, "Don't worry Crystal we don't speak in tongues. We do have a Holy Day on Pentecost. We gather together and have a sermon and we don't work. The spring and summer Holy Days as you can see have been fulfilled in that we see what happened and why those days exist. Those are days we look back on. The fall Holy Days have not been fulfilled yet. We don't know what will happen to fulfill those days. Just as in Jesus' day the people didn't know who or how Jesus would come. Some people couldn't accept Jesus because he didn't come the way they thought he should come. They mixed up his first coming with his second coming. In the same way we should not get too stuck on our own ideas as to what will happen, but know what the Bible says so we will recognize it when it does happen. Till then we will continue to keep God's Holy Days as the Bible says we should."

Martha says, "With that we shall explore what the fall days are. **Leviticus 23:23-25 NLT - 23 The LORD said to Moses, 24 'Give the following instructions to the people of Israel. On the first day of the appointed month in early autumn, you are to observe a day of complete rest. It will be an official day for holy assembly, a day commemorated with loud blasts of a trumpet.**

25 You must do no ordinary work on that day. Instead, you are to present special gifts to the LORD.'"

Martha continues, "This we call 'The Feast of Trumpets'. This is the day that predicts a day of warning. A trumpet call to war, if you like. It is held on the first day of the Jewish calendar's seventh month. As we see in Young's Literal Translation. **Leviticus 23:24-25 YLT - 24 Speak unto the sons of Israel, saying, 'n the seventh month, on the first of the month, ye have a Sabbath, a memorial of shouting,**

a holy convocation; 25 ye do no servile work, and ye have brought near a fire-offering to Jehovah.'"

Rachel says, "We bring an offering of money because coins, at sometime in their existence, has to go through a fire to be made, therefore, it is our closest form of an offering made by fire."

Lisa says, "If Passover is in April then the seventh month would be October. Right?"

Martha explains, "Sometimes it's in October and sometimes it's in September. Our calendar runs according to the sun. The Hebrew calendar runs according to the moon. A month goes from one new moon to the next new moon. Every three to four years they have to put a whole extra month in. We have our leap year where we add a day. Their leap year adds a whole month. If you're interested, you should look up the Hebrew calendar on the internet."

Lisa says, "I will, thank you."

Becky asks, "What's next?"

Martha says, "The Day Of Atonement. On this day we do not eat or drink from sundown the night before, until sundown that day. Lets read it. **Leviticus 23:26-32 NLT - 26 Then the LORD said to Moses, 27 'Be careful to celebrate the Day of Atonement on the tenth day of that same month--nine days after the Festival of Trumpets. You must observe it as an official day for holy assembly, a day to deny yourselves and present special gifts to the LORD. 28 Do not work during that entire day because it is the Day of Atonement, when offerings of purification are made for you, making you right with the LORD your God. 29 All who do not deny themselves that day will be cut off**

from God's people. 30 And I will destroy anyone among you who does any work on that day. 31 You must not do any work at all! This is a permanent law for you, and it must be observed from generation to generation wherever you live. 32 This will be a Sabbath day of complete rest for you, and on that day you must deny yourselves. This day of rest will begin at sundown on the ninth day of the month and extend until sundown on the tenth day.'

Rachel continues, "This is a day of coming back to the Lord. A day to recommit ourselves to God and his ways. They used to have a long drawn out ceremony involving two goats. Today we fast and we have our own ceremony. It gets involved. Not all Sabbath keeping churches follow the same rituals for each Holy Day. We can only tell you what we do on each Holy Day, though the Bible is specific on what they did back then. He (God) leaves it up to us to decide how we honor him on his days. As long as we don't follow what the world does to honor him. That will be a good study for next week's study."

Martha says, "Good, it looks like we have our next study subject. Our last two Holy Days are as follows. **Leviticus 23:33-44 NLT - 33 And the LORD said to Moses, 34 'Give the following instructions to the people of Israel. Begin celebrating the Festival of Shelters on the fifteenth day of the appointed month--five days after the Day of Atonement. This festival to the LORD will last for seven days. 35 On the first day of the festival you must proclaim an official day for holy assembly, when you do no ordinary work. 36 For seven days you must present special gifts to the LORD. The eighth day is another**

holy day on which you present your special gifts to the LORD. This will be a solemn occasion, and no ordinary work may be done that day. 37 (These are the LORD's appointed festivals. Celebrate them each year as official days for holy assembly by presenting special gifts to the LORD--burnt offerings, grain offerings, sacrifices, and liquid offerings--each on its proper day. 38 These festivals must be observed in addition to the LORD's regular Sabbath days, and the offerings are in addition to your personal gifts, the offerings you give to fulfill your vows, and the voluntary offerings you present to the LORD.) 39 Remember that this seven-day festival to the LORD--the Festival of Shelters--begins on the fifteenth day of the appointed month, after you have harvested all the produce of the land. The first day and the eighth day of the festival will be days of complete rest. 40 On the first day gather branches from magnificent trees--palm fronds, boughs from leafy trees, and willows that grow by the streams. Then celebrate with joy before the LORD your God for seven days. 41 You must observe this festival to the LORD for seven days every year. This is a permanent law for you, and it must be observed in the appointed month from generation to generation. 42 For seven days you must live outside in little shelters. All native-born Israelites must live in shelters. 43 This will remind each new generation of Israelites that I made their ancestors live in shelters when I rescued them from the land of Egypt. I am the LORD your God.' 44 So Moses gave the Israelites these instructions regarding the annual festivals of the LORD."

"The feast of tabernacles lasts for seven days and depicts two occasions, first the time Israel lived in the desert in tents for forty years, and second after Jesus comes again, we will live for a thousand years in peace and harmony with him," Rachel says.

Martha says, "The eighth day is 'The Last Great Day'. The day depicts the great judgment day. After that God himself, comes down in the new city, New Jerusalem talked about in **Revelations 21**. The eighth day is a Holy Day just as the first day is. This time is a Bible sanctioned vacation week. We are to save one tenth of our money for the year and spend it on this vacation. We are to have fun and share with our brothers in Christ. The Bible tells us to eat, drink and be merry at this time. It is a time of celebration."

Becky says, "So the Holy Days show us Gods plan for the world. From beginning to the end. And that's why we should keep them holy as God tells us to?"

Rachel says, "Yes, that's what we believe. And that's why we keep them in the way that we do."

Crystal says, "Ok, first the Bible says for Moses to tell the Israelites these are the instructions for the Israelites. Doesn't this mean it was just for the Jews? I'm not a Jew."

Martha states, "Let's let the Bible speak for itself. God said in **Jeremiah 31:33 NKJV - 33 But this is the covenant that I will make with the house of Israel after those days, says the LORD: I will put My law in their minds, and write it on their hearts; and I will be their God, and they shall be My people.**

2 Corinthians 6:16 NKJV - 16 And what agreement has the temple of God with idols? For you are the temple

of the living God. As God has said: 'I will dwell in them And walk among them. I will be their God, And they shall be My people.'

Hebrews 8:10 NKJV - 10 For this is the covenant that I will make with the house of Israel after those days, says the LORD: I will put My laws in their mind and write them on their hearts; and I will be their God, and they shall be My people.

Zechariah 8:8 NKJV - 8 I will bring them back, And they shall dwell in the midst of Jerusalem. They shall be My people And I will be their God, In truth and righteousness.

Revelation 21:3 NKJV - 3 And I heard a loud voice from heaven saying, 'Behold, the tabernacle of God is with men, and He will dwell with them, and they shall be His people. God Himself will be with them and be their God.'

Romans 11:11-24, 26 NKJV - 11 I say then, have they stumbled that they should fall? Certainly not! But through their fall, to provoke them to jealousy, salvation has come to the Gentiles. 12 Now if their fall is riches for the world, and their failure riches for the Gentiles, how much more their fullness! 13 For I speak to you Gentiles; inasmuch as I am an apostle to the Gentiles, I magnify my ministry, 14 if by any means I may provoke to jealousy those who are my flesh and save some of them. 15 For if their being cast away is the reconciling of the world, what will their acceptance be but life from the dead? 16 For if the first fruit is holy, the lump is also holy; and if the root is holy, so are the branches. 17 And if some of

**the branches were broken off, and you, being a wild olive tree, were grafted in among them, and with them became a partaker of the root and fatness of the olive tree, 18
do not boast against the branches. But if you do boast, remember that you do not support the root, but the root supports you. 19 You will say then, 'Branches were broken
off that I might be grafted in.' 20 Well said. Because of unbelief they were broken off, and you stand by faith. Do not be haughty, but fear. 21 For if God did not spare
the natural branches, He may not spare you either. 22
Therefore consider the goodness and severity of God: on those who fell, severity; but toward you, goodness, if you continue in His goodness. Otherwise you also will be cut
off. 23 And they also, if they do not continue in unbelief, will be grafted in, for God is able to graft them in again.
24 For if you were cut out of the olive tree which is wild by nature, and were grafted contrary to nature into a cultivated olive tree, how much more will these, who are natural branches, be grafted into their own olive tree? ...
26 And so all Israel will be saved, as it is written: 'The Deliverer will come out of Zion, And He will turn away ungodliness from Jacob.'**

So you see God calls Israel his chosen people, then he said he grafted in the gentiles so that they are now his chosen people also. If we believe in Jesus we are now God's children and adopted Israelites. Therefore what is good for them is also good for us. Understand?" Martha asks.

Crystal says, " I guess I understand."

Rachel asks, "You do want God to say to you,'I will be your God and you will be my person,' right?"

"Well, yeah, of course," Crystal says, "Who wouldn't?"

"In that case you should want to do what God says to do. When he talks to Israel consider it the same as if he were talking to you. In that way we are all Israelites," Rachel explains.

"Ok, I get it now." Crystal says. "So where does Christmas fit into all of this?"

Just then Bob sticks his head in the door and says, "Lunch time ladies"

Martha says, "We will have to cover that next week, I'm afraid."

They all head out for lunch and the rest of the fabulous Sabbath day's rest.

-10-

Becky is having a hard time keeping her mind on her job. All she can think about is what she has been learning at church. She and Lisa talk about it at lunch all the time. But Lisa seems to be able to concentrate on work better then Becky. And Becky is starting to feel that she is meant for something other than this job.

"I wish we would go back to the Wednesday study nights like we were doing in the beginning," Becky tells Lisa.

"Yeah, me too, kind of," Lisa confesses.

Becky asks, "But?"

"What?" Lisa asks.

"I get the feeling there's a 'but' in there," Becky says.

Lisa confesses, "Ok, but going to the Wednesday get-togethers were a bit hard for me. Elisa and Forman keep me really busy. But I do miss the Wednesday night Bible study. Oh, by the way, I think Forman is almost ready to come with me to church. I tell him everything I learn when I get home, but I will need your help. You know how he likes to be the center of attention."

"Yes," Becky says.

"Well, when he comes can you just pour on the charm. You know, make him feel like a rock star or like you really, really want him to be there," Lisa asks.

"Sure I can do that, just for you," Becky assures Lisa.

Sabbath finally comes, but Forman isn't there.

Becky asks Lisa, "Couldn't talk Forman into coming?"

"No, not yet, but he is weakening. I'll get him here one day, you'll see," Lisa says.

The Ladies head to their Sabbath school class after breakfast.

Martha starts, "Last week we decided to cover what the Bible says about doing what other religions do to honor their gods. Let's start with the following scriptures, and where Christmas fits into it all."

She reads **"Deuteronomy 12:4 NLT - 4 Do not worship the LORD your God in the way these pagan peoples worship their gods.**

"Deuteronomy 12:30-32 NLT - 30 do not fall into the trap of following their customs and worshiping their gods. Do not inquire about their gods, saying, 'How do these nations worship their gods? I want to follow their example.' 31 You must not worship the LORD your God the way the other nations worship their gods, for they perform for their gods every detestable act that the LORD hates. They even burn their sons and daughters as sacrifices to their gods. 32 So be careful to obey all the commands I give you. You must not add anything to them or subtract anything from them."

Martha continues, "So you see we are not to look at other religions and say 'let's honor God the same way these people

honor their gods.' The Bible says that is wrong. Crystal, you want to know about Christmas. Let's look at something else the Bible says about that. **Jeremiah 10:2-4 NLT - 2**
This is what the LORD says: 'Do not act like the other nations, who try to read their future in the stars. Do not be afraid of their predictions, even though other nations are terrified by them. 3 Their ways are futile and foolish.
They cut down a tree, and a craftsman carves an idol. 4
They decorate it with gold and silver and then fasten it securely with hammer and nails so it won't fall over.'"

"This is how the New King James puts it," Rachel says, "**Jeremiah 10:2-4 NKJV - 2 Thus says the LORD: 'Do not learn the way of the Gentiles; Do not be dismayed at the signs of heaven, For the Gentiles are dismayed at**
them. 3 For the customs of the peoples are futile; For one cuts a tree from the forest, The work of the hands of
the workman, with the ax. 4 They decorate it with silver and gold; They fasten it with nails and hammers So that it will not topple.' This sounds like what people do with a Christmas tree to me."

Martha continues, "Christmas, originally Christ's Mass is clearly a Catholic invention. This is a brief history of Christmas. Long before Christ came into this world the pagans celebrated the winter solstice and one or more of their gods' birthday, with running in the streets and looting and all kinds of ruckus behavior, while decent people hid in their houses. When Constantine wanted to unite his kingdom, he decided to combine the two religions with no regard to what the Bible says about not doing that, and declared the ancient pagan holiday of worshiping the sun and its return along with the birth of our Lord Jesus. Thus Christmas was born. So I ask you what do all of the lights and decorations, the exchanging of gifts and the greed which that instills, have to do with the birth of Jesus? Yes, the wise men came and gave gifts to the new born king, but they didn't come and stand before him and exchange gifts among themselves and leave without giving anything to Jesus. If you really wanted to give Jesus a gift, you would give the church a gift not each other. But of course people can justify anything they want to do. I'm not saying we can't give gifts to people. Giving is a very good thing to do. But we should do it out of love not because someone gave me a gift, so now I have to give them an even better gift. It soon becomes a competition. And there's that pesky little fact that Jesus wasn't born on or anywhere near Dec. 25. The Bible doesn't give us an exact birth date. If God wanted us to know he would have given us an exact date as he did for all of his other Holy Days. We don't even know if they celebrated birthdays back then. Except for some kings' birthdays mentioned in the Bible, we never hear about common people celebrating their birthdays. If they did or didn't really isn't what the issue is. I think it is a good thing to remember his birth. And if you put all of the clues together that are in the Bible you come up with a fall birth sometime on or between the Feast of Trumpets and the Feast of Tabernacles. A lot of church leaders put it on the first day of the Feast of Tabernacles. If you go back to the Holy Days and the plan God sets out for man, the first day of Tabernacles depicts when Jesus returns to this world to be with his people. So why wouldn't he come the first time then, too?" Martha finishes.

Rachel says, "I did a rather extensive study on that and everything I found points to a 'first day of Tabernacles birth date. I looked at all of the clues that the Bible gives. I even double checked it with the clues given in some of the books of the Bible that were dropped by the official Bible coordinators. And it still came out to a fall birth. The closest thing to Dec 25 is that could have been when Jesus was conceived. But even that is a guess. We won't know for sure until we see him when he comes back, and we can ask him."

Martha states, "We can speculate all we want. But the truth is, if God had wanted us to know, he would have told us. I think he didn't want his birthday to become the circus that the world has turned Christmas into."

Rachel says, "It is the tradition of *this church* to read the story of his birth as stated in Luke and Matthew every year to start the Feast with. But we don't make a big deal of it. It's just a reading."

After listening to all of this, Crystal says, "How boring. You people take all the fun out of everything. You're as bad as the Jehovah Witnesses. I went to their church once, but when I learned they don't 'celebrate' anything, I said, No thank you."

Rachel says**,** "We celebrate all kinds of things, like the seven Biblical Holy Days, Our birthdays, Thanksgiving, the fourth of July. The one I think you will really like is the Feast of Tabernacles. It's a weeklong celebration, like a Bible sanctioned vacation. We are even told to save our money all year so we can spend it at the feast. There's nothing wrong with celebrating things. We just stay away from the ones that are Pagan rituals for honoring their gods like Easter, Christmas and Halloween,"

Crystal says, "Halloween? Wants wrong with Halloween? The church gave us that one to honor our dead."

Rachel says, "Again the Catholic church invented that one. The Bible never said to worship or honor the dead like that. It says,

Psalm 106:28-29 NLT - 28 Then our ancestors joined in the worship of Baal at Peor; they even ate sacrifices offered to the dead! 29 They angered the LORD with all these things, so a plague broke out among them.

Mark 12:27 NLT - 27 So he is the God of the living, not the dead. You have made a serious error."

Proverbs 8:36 NLT - 36 But those who miss me injure themselves. All who hate me love death."

Proverbs 14:12 NLT - 12 There is a path before each person that seems right, but it ends in death.

"Really, does it take that much to see the inherent evil that exists in Halloween?" Rachel asks.

"Colossians 3:5 NLT - 5 So put to death the sinful, earthly things lurking within you. Have nothing to do with sexual immorality, impurity, lust, and evil desires. Don't be greedy, for a greedy person is an idolater, worshiping the things of this world.

"What do people associate Halloween with? Witches, skeletons and death, zombies, the Devil. All evil things that the Bible warns us to stay away from.

"Leviticus 19:26 NLT - 26 Do not eat meat that has not been drained of its blood. Do not practice fortune-telling or witchcraft.

"Deuteronomy 18:10 NLT - 10 For example, never sacrifice your son or daughter as a burnt offering. And do not let your people practice fortune-telling, or use sorcery, or interpret omens, or engage in witchcraft,

"1 Samuel 15:23 NLT - 23 Rebellion is as sinful as witchcraft, and stubbornness as bad as worshiping idols. So because you have rejected the command of the LORD, he has rejected you as king.

"2 Chronicles 33:6 NLT - 6 Manasseh also sacrificed his own sons in the fire in the valley of Ben-Hinnom. He practiced sorcery, divination, and witchcraft, and he consulted with mediums and psychics. He did much that was evil in the LORD's sight, arousing his anger.

"Revelation 9:21 NLT - 21 And they did not repent of their murders or their witchcraft or their sexual immorality or their thefts.

"Revelation 21:8 NLT - 8 But cowards, unbelievers, the corrupt, murderers, the immoral, those who practice witchcraft, idol worshipers, and all liars--their fate is in the fiery lake of burning sulfur. This is the second death," Rachel concludes.

Crystal says, "Well, yes, but it's all in fun. It's all make believe. No one is seriously worshiping the dead or the devil. If anything, it is making fun of all of that."

Rachel says, "Seriously, do you want to be provoking the third most powerful being in the world? His power is just under the power of Jesus, who is right under God the Father. Thank God there is no power greater than God. The angels and the demons are pretty well matched up except, thank God, there are two angels to every demon. But we are definitely under Satan and his demons when it comes to power. It is only by the grace of God that Satan can't just wipe us all away. The Bible says in **Jeremiah 25:6 NLT - 6 Do not provoke my anger by worshiping idols you made with your own hands. Then I will not harm you.'**

Luke 4:7-12 NLT - 7(Satan said) 'I will give it all to you if you will worship me.' 8 Jesus replied, 'The Scriptures say, You must worship the LORD your God and serve only him.' 9 Then the devil took him to Jerusalem, to the highest point of the Temple, and said, 'If you are the Son of God, jump off! 10 For the Scriptures say, He will order his angels to protect and guard you. 11 And they will hold you up with their hands so you won't even hurt your foot on a stone.' 12 Jesus responded, 'The Scriptures also say, <u>You must not test the LORD your God.'</u>

"If Jesus wouldn't tempt, or test God, who are we to do so by keeping Halloween?"

Crystal just says, "Oh, never thought of that."

Martha suggests, "I think you should pray about it and decide for yourself. We all should pray about all of the pagan holidays and see what is right for us."

Lisa adds, **"Joshua 24:14-15 NLT - 14 "So fear the LORD and serve him wholeheartedly. Put away forever the idols your ancestors worshiped when they lived beyond the Euphrates River and in Egypt. Serve the LORD alone. 15 But if you refuse to serve the LORD, then choose today whom you will serve. Would you prefer the gods your ancestors served beyond the Euphrates? Or will it be the gods of the Amorites in whose land you now live? But as for me and my family, we will serve the LORD."**

"Thank you, Lisa. That does wrap up a lot of what we are trying to teach all of you," Martha says.

Becky asks, "What's next?

"What do you want to cover next?" Martha asks.

Lisa asks, "Something was mentioned about Hades and some kind of fire? Can we cover that?"

Martha says, "That is an excellent topic. Shall we cover what the bible says about Heaven and Hades and Death next?"

The ladies all agree, but before they can get into it, Bob announces, "Time is up."

Martha says, "Well, I guess we have our topic for next week."

The ladies file out for lunch, which seems to be Italian based and delicious as always. Crystal and Jeff corner Pat and Rachel to discuss the Holy Days versus the holidays. Lisa and Julie get together to watch their kids and talk mostly about the best way to get Lisa's husband to come to church. Julie suggests taking a plate of food home.

"The best way to a man's mind is through his stomach," Julie says.

Lisa says, "I thought that was his heart?"

"That too," Julie says and they both laugh. Lisa makes a plate to take home.

Becky finds herself sitting alone. She watches Tom as he circulates around the room. She is brought back to reality when Miss Marcie says, "He is something, isn't he?"

"He is so at home talking to everyone. So at ease. I admire him for that," Becky says half dreamily.

"Are you sure that's all it is?" Miss Marcie asks.

Becky, coming back to full consciousness says, "Of course, why do you ask?"

"Oh, no reason," Miss Marcie says.

The ladies go back to eating. When Miss Marcie says, "You have such pretty hair. You should let it grow out a little, not a lot, but a little longer. It would be very flattering if you did."

"You think so?" Becky says.

"Yes, it would be really cute. I used to be a hair dresser. Figuring out what would look good on a person according to the shape of their face and all was my particular talent," Miss Marcie informs Becky.

"Wow, I didn't know that. That's so cool. I think I will let it grow. Thank you," Becky says, "will you help me style it?"

"I haven't done that in a while, but for you I would be honored, besides I don't think it would take much to just get the right cut and let it do its own thing after that," Miss Marcie says.

"Thank you, now I'm excited to let it grow," Becky says.

Lunch is soon over and it is now time for the afternoon sermons to begin.

Tom is the speaker for the day and speaks on the subject titled, "The Shadow of Things to Come". After the sermon there is a lengthy discussion. But for some reason Becky has a hard time keeping her mind on the discussion. Her mind is wandering all over the place. She finds herself day dreaming about what it would be like to go on a date with Tom. Then she chastises herself for thinking of such a thing. When supper time comes around, Becky isn't feeling very well and goes home early. Lisa says she will come by later to check on her. Becky says, "Thanks," and drives home. She goes to bed as soon as she can after getting home. After a while she hears a knock and figures it's Lisa. Becky is surprised when she opens the door to find Tom standing there with a large grocery store bag in hand.

"Oh, hi, I was expecting Lisa. Why are you here?" Becky asks.

"Sorry, Lisa had to go home, Elisa wasn't feeling well. She asked me to come by and check on you. She told me you weren't feeling well either. I brought you some ginger ale, and some vegetable broth. And when you are feeling better there's some hardy vegetable soup, and a box of Kleenex," Tom says.

"Oh, that's so sweet of you. I hope Elisa is better soon. Do you want to come in?" Becky asks.

Tom replies, "No, I have to be going."

But at that very moment Becky runs to the bathroom to throw up in the toilet. Tom follows and ends up holding her head and then helping her to bed. He pores some ginger ale in a cup of ice and heats up the broth. Then takes it in to Becky and gets her to sip a little of both.

Becky weakly says, "I'm sorry, you are so sweet to take care of me like this".

"That's ok, I am a nurse, you know," Tom says.

"Yes, I remember," Becky says, perking up a little.

"Do you think you can get these down?" as he holds two Tylenol out to her. She takes the pills and a little ginger ale and swallows the pills.

"Thanks," Becky says as she lays back down. Tom goes out and cleans up the kitchen. Then he sticks his head in to say good bye but seeing that Becky is already asleep, he quietly leaves."

-11-

Sunday Becky is feeling better. She is sitting in her living room wrapped in a blanket sipping on some herbal tea, when a knock comes at her door. Becky both hopes and dreads that it might be Tom. She would love to see him again, but she looks terrible and doesn't want to see him looking like she does. The knock comes again and she gets up looks out her peep hole and is relieved to see Martha standing there. Becky opens the door and greets the motherly lady. Martha has a grocery bag with ginger ale, and herbal tea and a variety of soups and crackers.

Martha asks, "How are you feeling today?"

Becky answers, "Better today. At least I'm keeping down what I eat, so far."

Martha says, "That's good. Just sip on things and keep it light. You don't want to overdo it and throw your system into a relapse."

Becky simply states, "Yes ma'am."

Martha continues, "Tom called and asked me to come check on you. He said you were feeling pretty bad last night and he was concerned."

Becky smiles, "Really? He was concerned about me?"

Martha smiles to herself, shakes her head a bit and says, "Yes, he was and is concerned about you, and Elisa, too. He called Lisa to check on her. Appears there is a stomach bug going around. At least it's not food poisoning from something the two of you ate at church, or we all would be sick. Besides I don't think you and Elisa ate the same things, because you two are the only ones that got sick." Martha places the back of her hand on Becky's forehead and says, "No fever. That's good. Are you going to be ok here by yourself?"

"Yes, I'll be fine. Thank you for stopping by and for all the goodies."

Martha says, "Oh, I almost forgot. Here, take one of these every hour until you go to bed. You should feel better tomorrow. If not, then take one pill every four hours. I've never had anyone take more than two days to feel well. If you still feel sick then, you'd better get to a Doctor." Martha hands Becky the bottle of pills.

"What are they?' Becky asks.

Martha explains, "It's an herbal remedy I get from a vitamin shop close to my home. They are safe. I'm confident they will help you feel better soon."

"Ok, thank you." Becky says as she opens the bottle and swallows one of the pills.

"I have a question?" Becky says, "Can we have a short Bible study now? I really want to know more about Baptism, and is it really necessary?"

Martha says, "Sure, but I left my Bible at home."

Becky says, "That's ok, we can use my new tablet, I need to learn how to use it anyway."

"Ok," Martha says.

They look up the words baptize and baptized in the Bible app Martha installs on Becky's new tablet.

Martha reads, "**Matthew 3:1-3, 5-10 NLT - 1 In those days John the Baptist came to the Judean wilderness and began preaching. His message was, 2 "Repent of your sins and turn to God, for the Kingdom of Heaven is near." 3 The prophet Isaiah was speaking about John when he said, "He is a voice shouting in the wilderness, Prepare the way for the LORD's coming! Clear the road for him!' ... 5 People from Jerusalem and from all of Judea and all over the Jordan Valley went out to see and hear John. 6 And when they confessed their sins, he baptized them in the Jordan River. 7 But when he saw many Pharisees and Sadducees coming to watch him baptize, he denounced them. 'You brood of snakes!' he exclaimed. 'Who warned you to flee God's coming wrath? 8 Prove by the way you live that you have repented of your sins and turned to God. 9 Don't just say to each other, 'We're safe, for we are descendants of Abraham.' That means nothing, for I tell you, God can create children of Abraham from these very stones. 10 Even now the ax of God's judgment is poised, ready to sever the roots of the trees. Yes, every tree that does not produce good fruit will be chopped down and thrown into the fire.'**

Matthew 3:11 NKJV - 11 I indeed baptize you with water unto repentance, but He who is coming after me is mightier than I, whose sandals I am not worthy to carry. He will baptize you with the Holy Spirit and fire.

John 1:25-26, 33 NKJV - 25 And they asked him, saying, 'Why then do you baptize if you are not the Christ, nor

Elijah, nor the Prophet?' 26 John answered them, saying, 'I baptize with water, but there stands One among you whom you do not know. ... 33 I did not know Him, but He who sent me to baptize with water said to me, 'Upon whom you see the Spirit descending, and remaining on Him, this is He who baptizes with the Holy Spirit."

John 4:1-2 NLT - 1 Jesus knew the Pharisees had heard that he was baptizing and making more disciples than John 2 (though Jesus himself didn't baptize them--his disciples did).

Mark 16:16 NKJV - 16 "He who believes and is baptized will be saved; but he who does not believe will be condemned.

Acts 2:38 NKJV - 38 Then Peter said to them, 'Repent, and let every one of you be baptized in the name of Jesus Christ for the remission of sins; and you shall receive the gift of the Holy Spirit.'

Acts 8:14-17 NKJV - 14 Now when the apostles who were at Jerusalem heard that Samaria had received the word of God, they sent Peter and John to them, 15 who, when they had come down, prayed for them that they might receive the Holy Spirit. 16 For as yet He had fallen upon none of them. They had only been baptized in the name of the Lord Jesus. 17 Then they laid hands on them, and they received the Holy Spirit.

Acts 10:48 NKJV - 48 And he commanded them to be baptized in the name of the Lord. Then they asked him to stay a few days.

Romans 6:3 NKJV - 3 Or do you not know that as many of us as were baptized into Christ Jesus were baptized into His death?

1 Corinthians 12:13 NKJV - 13 For by one Spirit we were all baptized into one body--whether Jews or Greeks, whether slaves or free--and have all been made to drink into one Spirit.

Galatians 3:27 NKJV - 27 For as many of you as were baptized into Christ have put on Christ. 28 There is neither Jew nor Greek, there is neither slave nor free, there is neither male nor female; for you are all one in Christ Jesus. 29 And if you are Christ's, then you are Abraham's seed, and heirs according to the promise."

Martha continues, "There are more versus on baptism. But they get a bit redundant. I think we can see, from the ones I read, that being baptized is important. When you confess your sins and repent or as Jesus said 'repent and sin no more.' You accept God's free gift of salvation, and then we are to confess it in a public display by going forward in church. As Jesus tells us to do,

Matthew 10:32 Therefore whoever confesses Me before men, him I will also confess before My Father who is in heaven.

Romans 10:9 NKJV - 9 that if you confess with your mouth the Lord Jesus and believe in your heart that God has raised Him from the dead, you will be saved.

You are baptized by going under the water, by doing this you are symbolically dead and buried and by coming back up you are symbolically raised from the dead, or resurrected into Christ.

Romans 6:3 NKJV - 3 Or do you not know that as many of us as were baptized into Christ Jesus were <u>baptized into His death</u>?

Romans 6:4 NKJV - 4 Therefore we were buried with Him through baptism into death, that just as Christ was raised from the dead by the glory of the Father, even so we also should walk in newness of life.

Colossians 2:10-13 NKJV - 10 and you are complete in Him, who is the head of all principality and power. 11 In Him you were also circumcised with the circumcision made without hands, by putting off the body of the sins of the flesh, by the circumcision of Christ, 12 buried with Him in baptism, in which you also were raised with Him through faith in the working of God, who raised Him from the dead. 13 And you, being dead in your trespasses and the uncircumcision of your flesh, He has made a live together with Him, having forgiven you all trespasses,

Then hands are laid on you and you receive Gods Spirit, His Holy Spirit.

Acts 8:15-17 NKJV - 15 who, when they had come down, prayed for them that they might receive the Holy Spirit. 16 For as yet He had fallen upon none of them. They had only been baptized in the name of the Lord Jesus. 17 Then they laid hands on them, and they received the Holy Spirit.

The Holy Spirit is not a third person separate from God. No, the Holy Spirit is simply God's Spirit or a piece of God himself, living in you. But it's not all that clear as to who or what the Holy Spirit is, so some people think of it as a third person in the Godhead. Who am I to say they are wrong. I'm just saying that as far as we can perceive, we believe that the Holy spirit is simply the Spirit of God. God's Spirit definitely lives in us and points us in the direction God wants us to go in. Understand?" Martha finishes.

"I think so." Becky says. "Thank you for that."

"You are welcome. Thank you for asking. I am always willing to share what the Bible says. But now I have to leave. Feel better soon," Martha says as she goes out the door.

Becky starts feeling better shortly after Martha leaves. She dutifully takes the pills as directed, though she is unsure if it's the pills that are making her feel better, or if she would be feeling better on her own anyway.

By Monday morning she is feeling almost back to normal, but she calls in sick anyway. She is certain it will be ok. She hasn't taken a sick day since she started her job three years ago. In fact she hasn't even taken a vacation. "I deserve a day off," she tells herself. She calls work and tells Lisa she won't be coming in today. Lisa tells her, "Rest and feel better soon." Becky hangs up and thinks about going back to bed then realizes she really isn't sleepy, so she makes herself some tea and snuggles up on the couch and turns on the TV. She spends the morning half watching and half cat napping till around noon, when she decides she is actually getting quite hungry. She rummages around in her kitchen but can't find anything she really wants. She is deep in thought about what to do next, when she hears a knock at her door which makes her jump. "*Who can that be*?" she wonders. She peeks out the peep hole and sees Crystal at her door. "*Ugh, what does she want. I'm really not up for company,*" she thinks to herself, but opens the door anyway. "Crystal, hi. What brings you by?"

"I heard you weren't feeling well and thought you might be getting tired of soup by now, so I make you this." She hands Becky a hot casserole dish. "Keep the dish as long as you like. I can't stay. I've got a cake in the oven. Hope you feel better soon," Crystal says as she turns to leave.

Becky barely has time to thank Crystal before she leaves. Becky shuts the door and takes the dish to her table. She uncovers the casserole and smells something wonderful emanating from the dish. Becky grabs a spoon from the kitchen and digs in. She isn't completely sure what this delicious dish is, but it really hits the spot. After eating about half the casserole, she decides to call Crystal.

"Hello," Crystal says.

"Crystal, my goodness, your casserole is so good. But please tell me what it is," Becky bursts out.

"Oh, Becky, it's you. I couldn't imagine who was calling. The solicitors don't usually start calling until the evening," Crystal laughs.

"Sorry," Becky says, "I just had to call and thank you for this wonderful food. It's so good I almost ate the whole thing and now I'm really stuffed. Please tell me what this delicious thing is?"

"It's just a simple tuna casserole... Oh, I'm sorry, I forgot, you're a vegetarian now," Crystal apologizes.

"That's Ok, for something this good I'll make an exception. I haven't been a vegetarian for that long. But there is nothing simple about this dish, it's fantastic. Thank you so much. You must have read my mind. I really needed that," Becky raves.

Crystal is glowing with happiness that her new friend is so pleased with her cooking. "Thank you, it makes me feel good knowing you like it."

"Like it? No, love it. I can't thank you enough," Becky says.

"Well, you are very welcome," Crystal says, "next time I won't forget and make you something vegetarian, I promise. In fact I have the perfect thing in mind already."

Becky states, "What are you thinking of making? Oh, never mind, if you make it I know it will be out of this world wonderful."

"Thank you, and you will have to wait and see," Crystal says coyly then giggles.

"Oh you, you are such a tease," Becky giggles back.

The girls say goodbye and hang up. Becky goes to her kitchen and starts cleaning up. After the kitchen is cleared out and clean, she goes and vacuums her whole apartment. After her burst of energy, Becky is feeling exhausted and curls up in bed with a book she has been meaning to read. But a pang of guilt hits her for eating and enjoying the tuna casserole so much. "I don't even know if tuna is a clean fish or not," Becky confesses. She prays for forgiveness just in case. And immediately feels forgiven. She vows to herself not to break her conviction to be a vegetarian again. Then she falls asleep with her book laying beside her, still unread.

-12-

Tuesday morning Becky is refreshed and in good spirits when she gets to work, but the feeling doesn't last long when she sees her desk with a mountain of papers stacked on it.

Lisa comes up behind Becky, and says, "Don't worry about that. Your desk was just handy. It will all be gone shortly. You really missed quite an eventful day yesterday."

"Oh, what happened?" Becky asks.

"Well, the boss, Mr. James, held a meeting first thing and tells us he has acquired another store in town. This one is a clothing store or 'boutique' as he calls it. And that our office staff will be changing because of it. He has hired a girl to be our file clerk. She is a bubbly girl, right out of high school, named Veronica. She works part time, just four hours a day, but she is very good and fast. A bit hyper but that's a good thing because she gets a lot done while she is here. She is doing a complete over haul of our filing system. That's why there is a mountain of papers on your desk. She is putting a lot of it on micro film."

"Wow, it's about time. This sounds hopeful," Becky says.

Lisa says, "Wait, there's more. He told us he is appointing an office manager. The choice was between you and me, and he choose me."

"That's great! I'm so happy for you," Becky says with a huge smile on her face.

"Really, you're not upset you didn't get it?" Lisa asks surprised. "You were here first."

"Upset? No. You will make a much better office manager then I would. So what if I was here six months before you. You are still the better choice," Becky reassures her.

Lisa hugs Becky and says, "I am so glad you feel that way. That really takes a weight off of me. Oh, and…"

"There's more?" Becky says.

"Unfortunately, yes, Mr. James has hired his nephew, Scott, to help out in the office," Lisa says. "He said he had no choice. He had made a promise to his sister to give her son a job. He starts today. So we will see how much 'help' he is," Lisa says.

Becky shakes her head and looks at her desk. "So what am I supposed to do with this?"

Lisa looks at the desk and says, "Well, you can have my old desk. I'm moving to my own new office in here."

"Wow, this is nice. You really are moving up in the world. And if I get your desk, I am moving up too. I do like your desk better. It's that much further from the boss," Becky says as she smiles.

Lisa smiles back and the ladies go to their desks to start the day. It isn't long before Lisa is stopping by Becky's desk to introduce a bubbly young girl, "Becky, this is Veronica Star, our new file clerk. Veronica, this is Becky."

"Nice to meet you'" Veronica says. "I hate to meet and run, but I have a lot of work to do. I'm sure we will get along nicely."

Veronica zips around removing papers to a new piece of equipment that just sort of appeared. Becky tries to concentrate on her job at hand. Mostly Becky listens to the tapes Mr. James gives her, and then translates them into a legible letter to be either sent out or filed.

At lunch time Veronica leaves for the day. Becky gets a chance to ask Lisa what the machine is that Veronica is using.

"Oh, that's the microfilming machine. I don't know anything about it, but it will give us a lot more space in here when she is done," Lisa says.

Right after lunch Scott finally decides to show up. He pitters around looking like he is doing something, but really he isn't doing anything. After an hour he declares he is going on his break.

The ladies look at each other in surprise, "Break? What's a break?" Becky asks Lisa.

Lisa replies, "Who knows?"

They both shake their heads and go back to work. Later Becky finds Scott in an empty office at the computer playing a computer game. She shakes her head and goes to Lisa.

"I found Scott," she tells Lisa.

"Oh, where is he?" Lisa asks.

"He's in the empty sales office playing games on the computer," Becky says.

"Well, at least he is out of our way," Lisa says. "Let's just give him a simple task and see if he actually accomplishes anything, and until that office is needed he can stay in there."

Becky says, "That sounds good to me. I have the perfect thing for him."

Lisa says, "Good, give it to me and I will take it to him."

Becky finds one of Mr. James' tapes that isn't important and gives it to Lisa.

Lisa takes it and goes to find Scott.

"Scott, here you are. You know this old empty office is perfect for you. I think you should stay in here. Oh, and here is a tape for you to type up for Mr. James."

Scott says, "Thanks for the office. I guess it will do. The letter is on a tape? Who uses tape anymore? That's so last year. Ok, I will be glad to type that up tomorrow. It's quitting time now."

At that Scott waltzes out of the building. Again the ladies shake their heads and go back to work.

Becky wonders how long this guy is going to last.

Scott "works" on the tape for the next three days. It would take Becky about fifteen minutes to type it up, but it keeps him out of the way. When Scott finally brings Becky the typed version Friday afternoon, it is exactly as dictated with all of the "ums" and "yada yada's", and "so on and so forth's" in it. The letter is completely useless.

Becky tells Lisa, "Wow, this guy has no idea what this job is all about. He has to learn to type what the Boss means, not what he says."

"Yes, that is so true. There is a special talent for being able to decipher what is meant, not what is actually said on those tapes of his," Lisa adds, "a talent Scott does not possess, I'm afraid. No one is as good at that as you are, my friend Becky."

"Thank you, my friend and my new boss. I like having you as my boss. I know you will be fair and honest with all the people under you, no matter what. Friend or foe, all are equal in your eyes," Becky states.

"Thank you, that means a lot to me for you to say that," Lisa says with a smile.

Becky adds, "See you tonight at church for vespers?"

"No, not tonight, I can't, but definitely tomorrow morning, and I think Forman might come too, at least I hope so," Lisa says.

"Ok, see you tomorrow," Becky says as the two ladies leave the building for the weekend.

-13-

Becky is relieved that it is finally Sabbath morning. She is looking forward to a day of rest in the Lord. Things at work have gotten weird. She really needs to get back to what's really important. She feels a little regretful that she missed vespers last night. She was so tired after getting home from work she decided to lay down for just a minute and the next thing she knew it was 1:00 am. She got up changed into her pajamas, brushed her teeth and went back to bed.

Now it is morning and she is refreshed and ready to learn, and seeing Tom and all of her church family again isn't a bad thing either.

She gets to church just as all the others are getting there too. She says "Hi" to Julie Wilson, then sees Tom, she is about to go over and say, "Hi". She wants to tell him all about her week, when a beautiful young woman runs up to him and gives him a big hug, then the two of them head off arm in arm toward the church. At that moment Lisa calls Becky's name. She turns around to see Lisa and her husband, Forman. She runs over and gushes all over Forman, then takes his arm and they walk into the church. Forman has a big grin on his face, but Lisa is not looking very happy about her friend's obvious advances toward her husband. Becky is very attentive to Forman throughout breakfast and makes sure everyone notices. Lisa wants to talk to Becky alone but she doesn't get the chance, for now it is class time.

As soon as the five ladies are in the room, Martha calls for them to start. She says an opening prayer and begins, "Today we are going to learn about what the Bible says about Heaven and Hades and Death. Let's start with death."

Rachel begins, "The Bible never asks us to choose between heaven and Hades. No, it asks us to choose between life and death. That is everlasting life or everlasting death, or the second death, not everlasting torture.

John 5:24 NKJV - 24 Most assuredly, I say to you, he who hears My word and believes in Him who sent Me has everlasting life, and shall not come into judgment, but has passed from death into life.

To pass from death into life you have to first be dead.

Deuteronomy 30:19 NKJV - 19 I call heaven and earth as witnesses today against you, that I have set before you life and death, blessing and cursing; therefore choose life, that both you and your descendants may live;

1 Corinthians 3:22 NKJV - 22 whether Paul or Apollos or Cephas, or the world or life or death, or things present or things to come--all are yours.

If you look up 'choose Heaven or Hades (or that other word)' in the bible you will come up empty. And if you look up 'immortal soul' you will also find that those words are not in the bible," Rachel says. "The Bible tells us that death is the enemy. If we went to heaven immediately then death wouldn't be the enemy, it would be our friend.

1 Corinthians 15:26 NLT - 26 And the last enemy to be destroyed is death."

Martha takes over, "The first lie the Bible records is in Genesis spoken by the serpent to the woman. Let's see what God said first,:

Genesis 2: 17 but you must not eat from the tree of the knowledge of good and evil, for when you eat of it you will surely die.

Then the serpent said,

Genesis 3:1-4 NKJV - 1 Now the serpent was more cunning than any beast of the field which the LORD God had made. And he said to the woman, 'Has God indeed said, You shall not eat of every tree of the garden?' 2 And the woman said to the serpent, 'We may eat the fruit of the trees of the garden; 3 but of the fruit of the tree which is in the midst of the garden, God has said, You shall not eat it, nor shall you touch it, lest you die.' 4 Then the serpent said to the woman, '<u>You will not surely die.'</u>

Hebrews 9:27 NKJV - 27 And as it is appointed for all men to die once, but after this the judgment.

We are made from dust and we return to dust when we die."Martha reads on,

"Genesis 2:7 NLT - 7 Then the LORD God formed the man from the dust of the ground. He breathed the breath of life into the man's nostrils, and the man became a living person.

Genesis 3:19 NLT - 19 By the sweat of your brow will you have food to eat until you return to the ground from which you were made. For you were made from dust, and to dust you will return.

Psalm 90:3 NLT - 3 You turn people back to dust, saying, 'Return to dust, you mortals!'

Everyone will die once.

Hebrews 9:27 NLT - 27 And just as each person is destined to die once and after that comes judgment,

Except those who are alive when Christ returns. The ones that do not believe in him will be left on earth for the believers to come back and rule over. All of Jesus' followers will be resurrected when Jesus comes again. If we went to heaven right away upon our death, then there would be no reason for Jesus to come back and get us. Why resurrect someone that is already alive and in heaven?" Martha finishes.

Rachel says, "Really, if I'm in heaven hanging out with God and Jesus and all my friends and relatives, having the best time ever, why would I want to come back to earth, crawl back into a dead, decayed, stinky body, or pile of bones, just so I can be resurrected all over again and go back to where I was to begin with. That is just silly. I would be asking Jesus 'Why?'

The Bible says in, **1 Thessalonians 4:15-18 NKJV - 15 For this we say to you by the word of the Lord, that we who are alive and remain until the coming of the Lord will by no means precede those who are asleep. 16 For the Lord Himself will descend from heaven with a shout, with the voice of an archangel, and with the trumpet of God. And the dead in Christ will rise first. 17 Then we who are alive and remain shall be caught up together with them in the clouds to meet the Lord in the air. And thus we shall always be with the Lord. 18 Therefore comfort one another with these words.**

Even here we just go to the clouds to meet with Jesus. It doesn't say we go to God's Heaven," Rachel explains .

Martha reads," **Revelation 20:1-6 NKJV - 1 Then I saw an angel coming down from heaven, having the key to the bottomless pit and a great chain in his hand. 2 He laid hold of the dragon, that serpent of old, who is the Devil and Satan, and bound him for a thousand years; 3 and he cast him into the bottomless pit, and shut him up, and set a seal on him, so that he should deceive the nations no more till the thousand years were finished. But after these things he must be released for a little while. 4 And I saw thrones, and they sat on them, and judgment was committed to them. Then I saw the souls of those who had been beheaded for their witness to Jesus and for the word of God, who had not worshiped the beast or his image, and had not received his mark on their foreheads or on their hands. And they lived and reigned with Christ for a thousand years. 5 But the rest of the dead did not live again until the thousand years were finished. This is the first resurrection. 6 Blessed and holy is he who has part in the first resurrection. Over such the second death has no power, but they shall be priests of God and of Christ, and shall reign with Him a thousand years.**

We will live and reign with Christ on earth, governing the people that are left behind. They are still mortal people that live on the earth They are not changed, because of their unbelief. We are to show them God and Jesus' way without Satan there to deceive anyone for a thousand years. Then Satan will be released to deceive again, then there will be a great war and Satan will be defeated again, but this time forever," Martha finishes.

Rachel continues, "All men at this time are the same in Gods eyes. We all have the same chance and the same choice, to choose life or death."

She reads, "**Ecclesiastes 9:2-6 NKJV - 2 All things come alike to all: One event happens to the righteous and the wicked; To the good, the clean, and the unclean; To him who sacrifices and him who does not sacrifice. As is the good, so is the sinner; He who takes an oath as he who fears an oath. 3 This is an evil in all that is done under the sun: that one thing happens to all. Truly the hearts of the sons of men are full of evil; madness is in their hearts while they live, and after that they go to the dead. 4 But for him who is joined to all the living there is hope, for a living dog is better than a dead lion. 5 For the living know that they will die; But the dead know nothing, And they have no more reward, For the memory of them is forgotten. 6 Also their love, their hatred, and their envy have now perished; Nevermore will they have a share in anything done under the sun.**

Colossians 3:11 NKJV - 11 there is neither Greek nor Jew, circumcised nor uncircumcised, barbarian, Scythian, slave nor free, but Christ is all and in all.

Deuteronomy 30:15 NKJV - 15 "See, I have set before you today life and good, or death and evil,

Psalm 89:48 NKJV - 48 What man can live and not see death? Can he deliver his life from the power of the grave?

Jeremiah 21:8 NKJV - 8 Now you shall say to this people, 'Thus says the LORD: Behold, I set before you the way of life and the way of death.'

John 5:24 NKJV - 24 Most assuredly, I say to you, he who hears My word and believes in Him who sent Me has everlasting life, and shall not come into judgment, but has passed from death into life.

How can you pass from death into life if you never died?"

Revelation 2:10 NKJV - 10 Do not fear any of those things which you are about to suffer. Indeed, the devil is about to throw some of you into prison, that you may be tested, and you will have tribulation ten days. Be faithful until death, and I will give you the crown of life.

There is no difference between us and animals, we all die the same death.

Psalm 49:20 NLT - 20 People who boast of their wealth don't understand; they will die, just like animals.

Ecclesiastes 3:18 I also thought, As for men, God tests them so that they may see that they are like the animals. Man's fate is like that of the animals; the same fate awaits them both: As one dies, so dies the other. All have the same breath (or spirit); Man has no advantage over the animal. Everything is meaningless. All go to the same place; all come from dust, and to dust all return," Rachel finishes.

Martha says, "We do not have an immortal soul, we have a mortal soul that can and does die. Jesus likened death to being in a very deep sleep. When is the last time you heard of someone under anesthesia getting up and walking out of a surgery room before the surgery is over?

John 11:11, 14 NKJV - 11 These things He said, and after that He said to them, 'Our friend Lazarus sleeps, but I go that I may wake him up.' ... 14 Then Jesus said to them plainly, 'Lazarus is dead.'

Acts 13:36 NKJV - 36 For David, after he had served his own generation by the will of God, fell asleep, was buried with his fathers, and saw corruption;

1 Corinthians 11:30 NKJV - 30 For this reason many are weak and sick among you, and many sleep.

1 Corinthians 15:18, 20 NKJV - 18 Then also those who have fallen asleep in Christ have perished. ... 20 But now Christ is risen from the dead, and has become the first fruits of those who have fallen asleep.

1 Corinthians 15:51 NKJV - 51 Behold, I tell you a mystery: We shall not all sleep, but we shall all be changed--

Ephesians 5:14 NKJV - 14 Therefore He says: 'Awake, you who sleep, Arise from the dead, And Christ will give you light.'

Romans 8:11 NKJV - 11 But if the Spirit of Him who raised Jesus from the dead dwells in you, He who raised Christ from the dead will also give life to your mortal bodies through His Spirit who dwells in you.

1 Corinthians 15:53-54 NKJV - 53 For this corruptible must put on incorruption, and this mortal must put on immortality. 54 So when this corruptible has put on incorruption, and this mortal has put on immortality, then shall be brought to pass the saying that is written: 'Death is swallowed up in victory.'

2 Corinthians 4:11 NKJV - 11 For we who live are always delivered to death for Jesus' sake, that the life of Jesus also may be manifested in our mortal flesh.

So we came from dust and we return to the dust just like all animals, when we die."

Martha is about to continue when Crystal asks, "What about our souls, our spirits. Don't they go to heaven or that other place?"

Crystal reads, **"Ecclesiastes 12:7 For then the dust will return to the earth, and the spirit will return to God who gave it."**

Rachel says; "The word that is translated 'spirit' here actually means breath, or air. So our bodies go to the ground and our breath goes to God who gave it. But I agree that 'something' that makes us us, I hope, goes somewhere to be kept safe and intact, call it our spirit or our soul. I want to be me when Christ returns to resurrect me and not just some random look alike. But the Bible says, The dead know not anything.

Ecclesiastes 9:5 NLT - 5 The living at least know they will die, <u>but the dead know nothing.</u> They have no further reward, nor are they remembered.

So, however God keeps my soul, my essence of who I am, I believe it will be unconscious and unaware of anything. But I trust it will still be me and not a robot or look alike. This is where hope and faith comes in."

"Let's see what the Bible says," Martha says. "Heaven is mentioned in the Bible 458 times from Genesis to Revelations. It talks about the stars in heaven and God in heaven and angels in heaven, but nothing about people being in heaven.

Genesis 27:28 NLT - 28 From the dew of heaven and the richness of the earth, may God always give you abundant harvests of grain and bountiful new wine.

Genesis 28:12 NLT - 12 As he slept, he dreamed of a stairway that reached from the earth up to heaven. And he saw the angels of God going up and down the stairway.

Isaiah 33:5 NLT - 5 Though the LORD is very great and lives in heaven, he will make Jerusalem his home of justice and righteousness.

Daniel 4:13 NLT - 13 Then as I lay there dreaming, I saw a messenger, a holy one, coming down from heaven.

Micah 1:3 NLT - 3 Look! The LORD is coming! He leaves his throne in heaven and tramples the heights of the earth.

Matthew 19:21 NLT - 21 Jesus told him, 'If you want to be perfect, go and sell all your possessions and give the money to the poor, and you will have treasure in heaven. Then come, follow me.'

We have treasure stored in heaven where it is safe. When Jesus returns our treasure or reward will be with him.

Isaiah 40:10 NLT - 10 Yes, the Sovereign LORD is coming in power. He will rule with a powerful arm. See, he brings his reward with him as he comes.

Isaiah 62:11 NLT - 11 The LORD has sent this message to every land: 'Tell the people of Israel, Look, your Savior is coming. See, he brings his reward with him as he comes,'
" Martha concludes.

Rachel takes over and says, "I can't find anything here about people going to heaven, I'll try 'soul goes to heaven'. Nope, nothing.

1 Corinthians 15:52 NLT - 52 It will happen in a moment, in the blink of an eye, when the last trumpet is blown. For when the trumpet sounds, those who have died will be raised to live forever. And we who are living will also be transformed.

1 Corinthians 1:8 NLT - 8 He will keep you strong to the end so that you will be free from all blame on the day when our Lord Jesus Christ returns.

Philippians 1:6 NLT - 6 And I am certain that God, who began the good work within you, will continue his work until it is finally finished on the day when Christ Jesus returns.

1 Thessalonians 5:10 NLT - 10 Christ died for us so that, whether we are dead or alive when he returns, we can live with him forever.

1 John 2:28 NLT - 28 And now, dear children, remain in fellowship with Christ so that when he returns, you will be full of courage and not shrink back from him in shame.

1 John 3:2 - Beloved, now we are children of God; and it has not yet been revealed what we shall be, but we know that when He is revealed, we shall be like Him, for we shall see Him as He is.

Revelation 10:7 NLT - 7 When the seventh angel blows his trumpet, God's mysterious plan will be fulfilled. It will happen just as he announced it to his servants the prophets.

Revelation 14:13 And I heard a voice from heaven saying, 'Write this down: Blessed are those who die in the Lord from now on. Yes, says the Spirit, they are blessed

indeed, for they will rest from their hard work; for their good deeds follow them!' 14 Then I saw a white cloud, and seated on the cloud was someone like the Son of Man. He had a gold crown on his head and a sharp sickle in his hand. 15 Then another angel came from the Temple and shouted to the one sitting on the cloud, 'Swing the sickle, for the time of harvest has come; the crop on earth is ripe.' 16 So the one sitting on the cloud swung his sickle over the earth, and the whole earth was harvested.

Revelation 19:7, 9, 11-14, 16, 20 NLT - 7 Let us be glad and rejoice, and let us give honor to him. For the time has come for the wedding feast of the Lamb, and his bride has prepared herself. ... 9 And the angel said to me, 'Write this: Blessed are those who are invited to the wedding feast of the Lamb.' And he added, 'These are true words that come from God.' ... 11 Then I saw heaven opened, and a white horse was standing there. Its rider was named Faithful and True, for he judges fairly and wages a righteous war. 12 His eyes were like flames of fire, and on his head were many crowns. A name was written on him that no one understood except himself. 13 He wore a robe dipped in blood, and his title was the Word of God. 14 The armies of heaven, dressed in the finest of pure white linen, followed him on white horses. ... 16 On his robe at his thigh was written this title: King of all kings and Lord of all lords. ... 20 And the beast was captured, and with him the false prophet who did mighty miracles on behalf of the beast--miracles that deceived all who had accepted the mark of the beast and who worshiped his statue. Both

the beast and his false prophet were thrown alive into the fiery lake of burning sulfur.

Revelation 20:2-8, 10-15 NLT - 2 He seized the dragon--that old serpent, who is the devil, Satan--and bound him in chains for a thousand years. 3 The angel threw him into the bottomless pit, which he then shut and locked so Satan could not deceive the nations anymore until the thousand years were finished. Afterward he must be released for a little while. 4 Then I saw thrones, and the people sitting on them had been given the authority to judge. And I saw the souls of those who had been beheaded for their testimony about Jesus and for proclaiming the word of God. They had not worshiped the beast or his statue, nor accepted his mark on their forehead or their hands. They all came to life again, and they reigned with Christ for a thousand years. 5 This is the first resurrection. (The rest of the dead did not come back to life until the thousand years had ended.) 6 Blessed and holy are those who share in the first resurrection. For them the second death holds no power, but they will be priests of God and of Christ and will reign with him a thousand years. 7 When the thousand years come to an end, Satan will be let out of his prison. 8 He will go out to deceive the nations--called Gog and Magog--in every corner of the earth. He will gather them together for battle--a mighty army, as numberless as sand along the seashore. ... 10 Then the devil, who had deceived them, was thrown into the fiery lake of burning sulfur, joining the beast and the false prophet. There they will be tormented day and night forever and ever. 11 And I saw a great white throne and the one sitting

on it. The earth and sky fled from his presence, but they found no place to hide. 12 I saw the dead, both great and small, standing before God's throne. And the books were opened, including the Book of Life. And the dead were judged according to what they had done, as recorded in the books. 13 The sea gave up its dead, and death and the grave gave up their dead. And all were judged according to their deeds. 14 Then death and the grave were thrown into the lake of fire. This lake of fire is the second death. 15 And anyone whose name was not found recorded in the Book of Life was thrown into the lake of fire.

Revelation 21:1-8, 25-27 NLT - 1 Then I saw a new heaven and a new earth, for the old heaven and the old earth had disappeared. And the sea was also gone. 2 And I saw the holy city, the new Jerusalem, coming down from God out of heaven like a bride beautifully dressed for her husband. 3 I heard a loud shout from the throne, saying, 'Look, God's home is now among his people! He will live with them, and they will be his people. God himself will be with them. 4 He will wipe every tear from their eyes, and there will be no more death or sorrow or crying or pain. All these things are gone forever.' 5 And the one sitting on the throne said, 'Look, I am making everything new!' And then he said to me, 'Write this down, for what I tell you is trustworthy and true.' 6 And he also said, 'It is finished! I am the Alpha and the Omega--the Beginning and the End. To all who are thirsty I will give freely from the springs of the water of life. 7 All who are victorious will inherit all these blessings, and I will be their God, and they will be my children. 8 But cowards, unbelievers,

the corrupt, murderers, the immoral, those who practice witchcraft, idol worshipers, and all liars--their fate is in the fiery lake of burning sulfur. This is the second death.' ... 25 Its gates will never be closed at the end of day because there is no night there. 26 And all the nations will bring their glory and honor into the city. 27 Nothing evil will be allowed to enter, nor anyone who practices shameful idolatry and dishonesty--but only those whose names are written in the Lamb's Book of Life.

Revelation 21 plainly says that our heaven is right here on earth. And after the end of it all God will be here among us forever. That's pretty exciting don't you think?" Rachel ends.

Becky says, "let me see if I got this right. Mainstream religions say we go to heaven or hades when we die. And there are scriptures that seem to support that. But if that were true, why aren't Christians lining up to be euthanized so they can get to heaven faster? Most people fear death, yet they claim they are Christians and believe they are going to heaven. People that are not Christians probably don't believe in heaven or hades anyway, so I can see why they wouldn't line up to be killed. This church believes that when we die, we just die, just like it looks like we do. That our bodies go to the grave and decay, and our souls go to some kind of 'cold storage' where it waits until Jesus returns. Then God's people are resurrected and changed from mortal to immortal, meet Jesus in the clouds, come back to earth and live with Jesus for a thousand years. Ruling over and teaching the mortal people left on earth. After the thousand years have ended, Satan is released to deceive the people again and the war of Armageddon is fought and Satan and all of his angels are thrown into the lake of fire. Then the unjust are resurrected to be judged. Some may repent and follow God, but the ones that don't, the ones that still follow Satan, are destroyed in a permanent death never to be remembered ever again. Satan and his angels may or may not be destroyed, but they will never again be heard from or remembered again. From the righteous person that dies perspective, they close their eyes in death and the next second Jesus is telling them to wake up and come meet him in the air because there is no time in death, even if they have been dead for thousands of years. After meeting Jesus in the air, they come back down to earth to rule with Christ for one thousand years, and then forever be with our Father God here on a new remade earth. So though death is not something to fear, it's not something to pursue ether. Right?"

Martha says, "Yes that's it exactly and there are lots of scriptures that support that. We only covered a small amount of them."

Lisa says: "I get all of that but what about that Gehenna fire? Where does that fit in?"

Martha explains, "In Jerusalem they had a trash pit that was kept burning all the time. All of the trash and bodies of wild animals, etc., were thrown into this forever burning fire to be disposed of. This 'dump' was called Gehenna. In the Bible where it says Hades it usually means either the grave or the ever burning dump of the Gehenna fire."

"Oh," Lisa says. "That makes sense. So that's where the 'Lake of fire' comes from."

Crystal says, "But on the cross Jesus says to the other guy being crucified 'today you will be with me in paradise'. How does that fit in with all of this?"

Rachel takes this one, "In the Hebrew written language there were no punctuations, so Jesus probably meant I'm telling you today, that (when I come back) you will be with me in paradise. Otherwise you are calling Jesus a liar."

"How's that?" Crystal asks bewildered.

Rachel continues; "Because Jesus didn't go to heaven or paradise that day. He went to the grave. Even if you believe what some mainstreamers think that he went to 'the underworld' to fight for us, he still didn't go to heaven or paradise that day."

"Oh," Crystal says, "That makes sense. Jesus couldn't lie even on the cross."

With that, time is up and the ladies all go out for lunch.

Lisa and Becky meet up with Forman. Becky is feeling a bit guilty about acting like such a school girl during breakfast. But when she sees Tom and his "girlfriend," she just can't take it any longer. She excuses herself and leaves. She doesn't want to go right home. So she goes to a park on the other side of the lake where she can think. She gets out to go for a walk along one of the many trails. She leaves her cell phone in the car and locks it. She aimlessly walks and thinks, "What is wrong with me. I made an absolute fool of myself at church. *But Lisa told you to make a fuss over Forman, and he was eating it up.* Yea, and now he probably thinks I like him or something. Gross, he is so not my type, and Lisa is my best friend. I would never hurt her. So why did I do that? *Because he was convenient. You had to show Tom he's not the only one that can get a new 'friend' so fast, and so cute.* So what if Tom has a girlfriend, I'm not looking for a man to be in my life. Why am I feeling so jealous? *Because he is so cute and you really thought there was something brewing there.* Well, there obviously isn't anything "brewing" between us, at least not as far as he is concerned. I will have to apologize to Lisa on Monday. I can't believe I acted so badly with Forman. I certainly am not interested in him. Wow, what am I going to do. Becky spends a long time hanging out at the park. She finally heads back to her car and goes home. She spends Sunday cleaning her apartment and doing laundry. She thought she heard her phone ring once or twice, but she ignored it.

On Monday she really wants to talk to Lisa, but things are so hectic they just don't get the chance. It's not until Tuesday that they finally get the chance to talk.

"What was that all about last Sabbath with you and Forman?" Lisa attacks.

Becky instinctively lashes back, "You told me to make a fuss over him. I was just doing what you asked me to do."

"I said make a fuss, you know, be nice, not throw yourself at him like a common hussy. You were acting like a tramp. Everyone was staring. I was so embarrassed we left right after you did," Lisa counters.

Becky is hurt and frustrated and counters with, "I can see this conversation isn't going anywhere." Becky gets up and says as she is leaving, "Let me know when you are ready to discuss this like a grownup."

Lisa and Becky both leave the area in opposite directions. They don't talk again.

They avoid each other on Wednesday. Thursday Becky is late getting to work, as she is settling down to work, Lisa comes out of Mr. James' office, when she sees Becky she stammers out, "Oh, Becky, I'm so sorry," and runs off bursting into tears.

As Becky is staring after her wondering, "*What In the world was that about?*" Mr. James calls her into his office.

"Yes, sir," Becky says.

"Sit down," He says. Becky sits.

Mr. James continues, "That big business deal I had to buy that boutique fell through and now I have too many people working here, so I have to let someone go. I can't lay off Scott. He is doing so well and I promised my sister. And Veronica is only part time, so she is actually not costing me that much. So that leaves you or Lisa." Becky is thinking, "*No, you're not going to get rid of Lisa. That must be why she was crying. Poor Lisa*". Mr. James says, "I'm sorry Becky, despite Lisa's objections, I'm going to have to let you go. Clean out your desk. Today is your last day." He then dismisses her with a wave of his hand and pretends to be busy doing something at his desk.

Becky walks out in a daze. Lisa is in her office and Becky walks in and looks at her friend who still has puffy red eyes from crying.

"I have a lot to say, so please don't throw me out. I'm touched that you are more upset than I am at this point. I guess I'm too stunned to be upset. Second I don't want to leave with us fighting. I was an absolute idiot and a fool last Sabbath. I'm very sorry for acting like that. I have no interest in Forman, and I wouldn't hurt you like that even if I was interested. But when I saw Tom with that 'girl' I just lost it and wanted to make him feel just as jealous as I felt. So please, forgive me," Becky says.

Lisa smiles and says "No, it was all my fault. I practically threw Forman into your arms, then got jealous myself. That was pretty silly of me. I know you better than that. And I know Forman. Even he was a little shocked at you. He said he enjoyed church and wants to go back to church next week, but you have to promise not to be so 'weird'. Those were his words. Just be yourself. Ok?"

Becky also smiles and says, "I promise to be myself and not act like a love sick school girl. Please tell Forman I'm sorry and why I did it. I hope he understands. I will apologize to him too the next time I see him, but explaining the whole 'crush' thing that would be a bit awkward. So please pave the way for me. Ok?"

"Sure, he is a reasonable man. I'm sure he will understand and forgive you. Besides I think he really was flattered by it all," Lisa smiling says. "We will all get a big laugh out of this one day."

"Yeah, you're probably right. It already seems pretty funny," Becky states.

"And I was surprised to see Tom with that girl too. I really thought the two of you would get together, but I guess not. I'm sorry. And now you are being laid off. What are you going to do now?" Lisa asks somberly.

Becky takes a big breath and says, "I have no Idea, but actually I feel sorry for you. You're the one who has to work with Scott. Good luck with that."

Both ladies laugh about that, then Lisa says, "You're right about that. I'm really going to miss you around here. But I hope I will get to see you at church every Sabbath."

Becky shrugs, "We'll see," she says.

Lisa says, "I hope you don't give up on the church and all that we learned just because you have a crush on the pastor and got your feelings hurt."

Becky states "It's not just that. I really embarrassed myself in front of everyone. I don't know if they can forgive me."

Lisa reassures her, "Girl, if I can forgive you, I'm sure everyone else will too. Just tell me you won't give up on the church, even if you go to a different Sabbath keeping church."

"Ok, I promise not to give up on the Sabbath. And I will keep in touch with you always," Becky promises.

At that Mr. James passes by and gives the ladies a look that says, "Becky, you need to leave now. You don't work here anymore."

Becky looks at him, then at Lisa, and says, "Well, I'd better get before he calls the police and has me removed."

"Yeah, you're right," Lisa says, and gets up and gives her friend a hug. "See you soon. Don't be a stranger, ok?"

"Ok, bye," Becky says and leaves the office for the last time.

-14-

When Becky gets home she decides she better look at her finances and figure out what she is going to do. With her last check from work she has just enough to either pay her rent for the next month or pay her car note and buy a few groceries. She opts for the car and food. She calls the apartment manager and tells him her story. He says, "Oh Becky, I'm sorry to hear that. But this is a business and if you can't pay, you will have to leave. I will be nice and forgo the usual 30 day notice and let you leave right away. Since rent is due tomorrow, we are even if you leave by then." Becky says, "Ok, I will be out by tomorrow." She sarcastically thinks "*nice man*". After hanging up, she starts removing her meager belongings and putting them in the car. Except for the bare essentials, she gets her car all packed. Everything fits but just barely. She sleeps later than she had planned. She dresses in her favorite old blue jeans and a tee-shirt. She puts the last of her stuff in the car and goes back in to see if she had forgotten anything. When her cell phone rings and it reminds her that she is glad she never got a home line, one less thing to have to worry about. She answers her phone and is surprised to hear Tom's voice.

"Becky, please come to the church. I really need your help with something," Tom pleads.

"Now?" Becky states surprised.

"Yes, right now, if you can," Tom sounds urgent.

Becky thinks, "Why not? It's not like I have anywhere else I have to be," though she is feeling a bit annoyed.

"Ok, I'll be there in five minutes," Becky tells him.

"Great!" Tom says, "See you soon," and hangs up before Becky can even say goodbye.

Becky looks at her phone and wonders, "*What's that all about? Only one way to find out.*" She goes to the office and turns in her apartment key and mail box key. Then she gets in her car and heads to the church. She thinks about stopping for breakfast, but realizes she doesn't have the money to spare. She will stop off at the store after she finds out what Tom wants.

When she gets to the church a few minutes later, Tom is in the yard waiting for her. He motions for he to park there in the driveway and not pull into the back. Becky stops and gets out. Tom takes her hands and leads her to the bench under the tree in the front yard. They both sit and Tom starts, "I have a great opportunity to go on a mission trip, basically around the world. It's what I have wanted to do for … well … forever. It's all expenses paid, and the opportunity of a life time. There is only one catch. I have to be married."

Becky breaks in and says, "Tom, really, I just lost my job and my apartment."

"That's great," Tom says smiling. Becky is starting to really get mad.

"And now you want me to help you get married to your girlfriend? Are you nuts?" Becky says angrily.

Tom is stunned, "What?... What Girlfriend?"

Becky says, "That girl that was hanging all over you last Sabbath."

"You mean Sara? I introduced her to the church," Tom says confused.

"I left before that," Becky explains, "I missed that."

"Oh, that was my niece, Sara. I haven't seen her in a long time. She was on her way to Alaska and wanted to see me before she and her husband left," Tom explains.

"Oh," Becky says, feeling pretty foolish.

Then Tom looks at her rather sternly and says, "And who are you to talk? You were hanging all over 'that guy' yourself? Who was he?"

"Uh, that is Lisa's husband, Forman. It was his first time to the church and Lisa wanted me to help make him feel at home. I guess I took it a little too far," Becky confesses.

"Ya think! …So no boyfriend?" Tom asks.

"No, no boyfriends," Becky states, "and You? No girlfriends?"

"No, no girlfriends," Tom says.

"Wow, I feel really stupid now," Becky says.

"Me too," Tom says. "But it is kind of funny, don't you think?"

They sit quietly for a bit, then Becky inquires, "So who are you going to marry so you can go on your dream mission?"

"Well,… You,… I hope? If you'll have me?" Tom says as he gets down on one knee.

"Me? Are you sure you want ME?' Becky stammers.

"Yes, I want you," Tom says still down on one knee.

Becky smiles and says, "Yes,.. Yes I will."

"Great," Tom says and they hug each other. "So let's go."

"What? Now?" Becky asks.

"Yes, I, we, have to be ready to go tomorrow," Tom says.

"Really? I know you didn't just learn about this today. You could have asked me earlier," Becky sternly says.

"Well, I only found out about it a week ago. I had applied for it six months ago, but I didn't know about the married part until last week when I got the confirmation. I was going to ask you last Sabbath, but then there was that whole thing with Forman and all. I tried to call you a few times during the week, but you never answered," Tom explains.

"Oh," Becky says, "Sorry but Now? I can't get married now, I'm in blue jeans. This is not how I pictured myself getting married," Becky says. "Besides there are two things I have to know first, and one thing I have to do."

"What is that?" Tom asks.

"First: Tell me, why me?" Becky asks.

Tom looks at her and asks, "Why did you say yes?"

Together they both say, "Because I love you."

They both smile and Tom says "Wow, you just made me the happiest man ever. What else?"

"This will sound weird but I don't know your last name," Becky confesses.

Tom says, "That's not weird, I just realized I don't know your last name either."

They both say in unison, "Watson. What? Your name is Watson too? Really?"

They both laugh, then Tom says well I guess that's good. You won't have to change your name on your license or your passport… Ugh, a pass port, we don't have time to get you a passport. Now what are we suppose to do?

"It's ok. I have a passport," Becky says.

"You do? Great!" Looking puzzled Tom asks, "Why do you have a passport?"

"About six months ago my apartment roommate suggested we go to Mexico during spring break. We had had a few drinks and it seemed like a good idea at the time. So we both went down and got our passports. That's when I decided never to drink again, or at least not get drunk. One, I really don't like it, and, two, I can be talked into doing really dumb things. I could have ended up with a tattoo or something worse than a passport. That was a weird day. Anyway, then all of this church stuff happened and Jennifer moved out and I pretty much forgot I even had it. I found it when I was packing my car and put it in my purse," Becky explains.

"Wow, God is good, He thinks of everything," Tom says, "Did you say you have everything you own, in your car right now?"

"Yes, I told you I lost my Job yesterday, and my apartment this morning," Becky says.

"Oh wow, Sweetheart, I'm so sorry," Tom says seriously. Then brightening up again he says. "But that means we are free to get married and go on our year long missionary trip. You can store all of your stuff, that is except for what you take with us on our trip, here at the church."

"What about my car? I still owe a lot of money on it," Becky says, "And what about your car?'

"I sold it," Tom says, "And all of my stuff is in the attic already. Bob said he would buy your car, well, it's more like a lease. You can get it back when we return."

"Oh," Becky says, "You were pretty d a r n sure I was going to say yes."

"No, I wasn't sure about anything, but I sure prayed you would. My trust is in God. I figured God would come up with some way for me to go, if that's what he wanted me to do. And I really wanted you to say yes, whether I went or not, because I've fallen head over heels in love with you. I liked you the first day we met and you so valiantly pulled out that bush. But that day I came over to take care of you when you were sick, that's the day when I fell in love with you, " Tom says dreamily as he thinks back. Then he snaps back to the present and asks, "You said there was something you wanted to do before we got married?"

"Yes," Becky says, and looks deeply into Tom's eyes. "Baptize me."

"You've never been baptized?" Tom asks, looking surprised.

"No, I just became a Christian, I was waiting to find the right church first," Becky says.

At that, Tom yells, "Martha, fill the tub in the back yard. We're going to have a baptism."

Suddenly Martha comes running out and says, "Did I just hear you say we're having a baptism? Right now? I thought we were having a wedding?"

"It's both." Tom says.

Martha hugs Becky and says, "Welcome to the family, my dear. I'll get everything ready, give me ten minutes." She turns to the house and yells, "Ladies, get ready. We're having a baptism!"

Becky hears other voices coming from inside the house. She looks at Tom and asks, "How many people are here?'

Tom counts on his fingers as he calls out names; "Well, there's Martha and her sister Clara, and Rachel, and Crystal. That's four. No, five, Miss Marcie is here too."

"Wait, Crystal is here? Well that explains why I didn't see her at the complex before I left," Becky says.

Just then a car drives up and Pat gets out. Tom says. "Oh, and Pat. That makes six. And me and you, of course, so eight."

Becky stares at Tom. Tom counters with, " Well, I had to be ready in case you said yes. The ladies all rallied around and are getting everything ready on very short notice. They were more sure you would say yes then I was, I think." And he laughs.

Just then Crystal comes out and grabs Becky by the arm and leads her inside saying, "Come on, we have to get you ready."

Becky dumbly follows where her friend leads her. A second later Crystal comes out and rummages through Becky's car. Grabs some clothes and yells at the house. "Got it." And rushes back in the house.

Tom walks around to the back yard and finds Pat filling the horse trough with water from the hose. Martha comes out every few minutes and dumps steaming pots of hot water into the trough. She puts her hand in the water shakes her head and goes back in, just to come out with more hot water. When the trough is almost full and Martha is satisfied the temperature is just right, Pat turns off the hose, turns to face the house and stands looking at the door. Tom stands on the other side of the trough and looks at the door as well. Then a procession of ladies walk out, first Martha, then Clara, then

Rachel, then Becky, closely followed by Crystal. Becky is wearing a black robe. Rachel and Crystal help Becky step into the trough and sit down, legs stretched out straight in front of her. Becky's robe turns blood red. Tom is handed a folded white handkerchief . Tom kneels down next to the trough and says, "We are here today, in front of these witnesses, to baptize Miss Becky Watson, not into any one church or congregation, but to baptize her into God's family.

Galatians 3:26-29 NKJV - 26 For you are all sons of God through faith in Christ Jesus. 27 For as many of you as were baptized into Christ have put on Christ. 28 There is neither Jew nor Greek, there is neither slave nor free, there is neither male nor female; for you are all one in Christ Jesus. 29 And if you are Christ's, then you are Abraham's seed, and heirs according to the promise."

He looks at Becky and asks, "Have you repented from all of your sins and are you resolved to go and 'sin no more' as Jesus has told us to do"?

"Yes," Becky says resolutely.

"Do you believe in God the Father? To have no other gods before him? Do you value his laws and strive to keep them, not to be saved but because you are saved?"

"Yes," Becky declares.

Tom continues, "And do you believe in God's only begotten Son, Jesus the Christ? That he came to save the world and not condemn it? And that he will return, in like manner, one day to collect us, his bride, to be with him forever?"

"Yes," Becky says.

"And do you believe in God's Spirit, that God's Holy Spirit will come live in you, that your body is now the temple of God and should be treated as such?" Tom finishes.

"Yes," Becky answers.

"Then I baptize you in the name of the Father, and His Son, and in His Spirit. As Jesus commanded his disciples to do in **Mathew 28:18-20**."

At that Tom puts the cloth over Beck's mouth and nose, and dunks her under the water, then immediately brings her back out again. Tom stands up and Pat and Tom help Becky out of the trough. Before Becky can take a step toward the church house everyone surrounds her and they put their hands on her and pray for her to be filled with God's Holy Spirit. As Becky opens her eyes after the prayer she notices that her robe that was black, then red, is now perfectly white.

The ladies lead Becky into the church house to start getting her ready for her wedding. Pat takes Tom to his car and drives away for a brief "bachelors party." Ok, it is just the two of them at a malt shop, but with all the hub-bub going on at the church, Pat thinks it best if the guys get out of the ladies way. If they are needed the ladies have their cell numbers. After finishing their malts the guys head to the barber shop and the rent-a-tux place. The ladies aren't the only ones that have to get ready. Then they go to Pat and Rachel's house to get Tom all "dolled up" as Pat's dad would have said. While Tom is getting dressed, Pat heads to the airport to pick up the surprise guests.

Meanwhile at the church, after getting Becky all dried off and half dressed, the ladies get Becky into a chair and Miss Marcie goes to work on Becky's hair, while Crystal and Rachel each take a hand and start doing an at-home manicure. Martha and Clara volunteer for feet and start on her pedicure. They paint her nails a pretty pastel pink. Lisa shows up with Elisa, Lisa takes over the hand Crystal is working on so she can start on Becky's makeup. Rachel takes off to start decorating the main room of the church. Soon other ladies from the church show up and help set things up for the wedding. Rachel let's everyone know that a reception will be held at her family's restaurant right after the wedding.

With strict instructions not to move while her polish dries, the ladies get their chance to get dressed. On such short notice Crystal has managed to get Lisa, Rachel and herself into closely matching powder blue dresses. Crystal is a natural at planning and executing parties and weddings. Even Elisa as the flower girl is dressed in a similar style and color dress.

Rachel brought her wedding dress, but Crystal says, "Rachel, darling, this dress is very beautiful, but it really is way too fancy for this wedding, I also brought my wedding dress which is pretty, but a little more understated."

Rachel replies, "They both are pretty and I see what you mean, but I think we should let Becky decide which one she wants to wear."

"Fair enough," Crystal says and goes to retrieve Becky.

"Becky, dear, we need you to come pick which dress you want to wear," Crystal says as she grabs Becky by the arm, careful not to mess up her polish, even though it is dry. Crystal is instinctively careful about things like that.

Becky is a bit overwhelmed, "Wow, I can't believe I get a choice. I just thought….well, I really haven't had any thoughts about what I am going to wear. I haven't gotten the chance to think about anything really. Everyone has been so fantastic and done everything, a girl can't ask for more."

Crystal leads Becky to the bedroom where the dresses are displayed.

Crystal's dress, on Crystal, is a mid calf length, because Crystal is quite a bit taller than Becky. On Becky it will be floor length. It is white satin, with some bead work around the modest V-neck, and around the short sleeves it is elegantly understated.

Rachel's dress is, of course, white, with a full satin skirt that spreads out forever. The kind of dress that fills up half the room with lots of petticoats under it to make it stand out. There are beads and rhinestones all over the whole dress with a lace covering that drags the ground. It is very beautiful and overdone the kind of dress royalty would wear in a wedding with two thousand invited guests. And even though Becky feels like Cinderella, Rachel's dress is a bit much.

Becky, not wanting to hurt Rachel's feelings says, "Rachel this dress is beyond beautiful, and I wish I could wear both dresses, but I have to choose one. And for this occasion I choose the less elaborate one."

Crystal says, "Yes," as she punches the air in victory.

Rachel says to Becky, "You made a good choice. I would have gone for the same one myself, if I were getting married here."

Crystal looks at Rachel with a "was that a dig?" kind of look, but then gets back in the moment and gets her dress and helps Becky into it. The dress is a little tight but not bad. And she looks awesome in it. The ladies carefully put the veil on Becky's head and cover her face. Then Becky stands back and looks at herself in the mirror.

Phones come out and pictures are taken. Both Crystal and Rachel say, "Becky, you are beautiful."

Becky holds back tears of sheer joy as she says, "I don't know how to thank you guys. All of this is so fairy-tale perfect. I could never have come up with anything so wonderful even if I had six months to plan it all. And you guys look fantastic too. How did you manage to come up with matching dresses? Don't tell me you went shopping while my nails were drying?"

Rachel says, "Don't you dare cry, you'll mess up your makeup."

Crystal giggles as Lisa walks in, also wearing a powder blue dress.

Becky looks at Lisa and says, "You too? Your dress is the same too."

Crystal explains, "It wasn't that hard, everyone has a powder blue dress somewhere in their closet. I just told them to get it out and bring it."

Just then Elisa comes in with a pair of white sandals in her hand and says, "You're not planning on getting married barefoot are you?"

Becky lifts her dress just a little and all the ladies laugh. Becky says, "Thank you, Elisa, and thanks for finding my sandals. I would hate to cover up these pretty toes with shoes. These sandals are perfect."

"No biggie, just thought you would want something on your feet. Saw those sandals and thought they were cute," Elisa says nonchalantly. She looks at Becky and says "Wow, you look beautiful."

Becky looks at Elisa and says, "So do you. I am told you are going to be my flower girl? I think I like junior brides maid better. You're much to grownup to be called a flower girl."

"Yeah, I like that too. I wanted to be a part of my Mom's best friend's wedding. Besides, you're my friend too," Elisa says.

"Thank you, that means a lot to me. You're both my friends. You're all my friends," Becky says getting emotional again.

Crystal sternly tells Becky, "Oh no, you are not going to cry. We don't have enough time for me to re-do your make up now." This makes Becky laugh instead.

Just then Becky's Mom walks in the door and says, "Becky, you're so beautiful. And here you are getting married. I didn't even know you had a boyfriend, let alone a fiancé?"

Becky looks at her Mom and says, "Neither did I."

"What?" Mrs. Watson says puzzled.

"Long story, Mom, I don't think I have time to tell you now," Becky says. "You look nice too."

Her Mom says, "Thank you. Oh yeah, they sent me in here to tell you all is ready."

At that Becky's Mom turns and hurries out to be seated.

The ladies file out the door. Elisa first, with her basket of flower pedals, to meet up with her escort, the ring bearer, who was suppose to be Ethan, but he refused so Jayden graciously said, "Ok," even though he thinks he is too old to be a ring bearer. Secretly he kind of likes Elisa, so it's not so bad.

Then Rachel, then Crystal, then the maid of honor, Lisa, and then Becky walks out to have her Dad take her arm.

"Daddy! Now this day is perfect," Becky whispers to her Dad. Her Dad turns to look at his beautiful daughter and smiles.

Martha plays the piano and her sister Clara sings.

The main room of the church has been transformed into a proper wedding chapel. The tables are gone and the chairs are all draped in white ribbon and lined up with an aisle down the middle. The room is full of people. Elisa scatters flower petals as she walks down the aisle with a slightly embarrassed Jayden by her side. The other ladies and their escorts file in behind as they proceed up the aisle to stand beside the podium. The men go to one side and the ladies on the other. As Becky enters, Martha plays the wedding march and everyone stands and turns to look at her. There is a man behind the podium that Becky does not recognize. She notes how handsome all the men look then she sees Tom in his tux looking so handsome her breath is taken away. She falls in love even more. She is surprised when the men sing a special song in perfect barber shop quartet style, with Tom singing a solo part. He is really good. They reach the front and her Dad gives her to Tom. Tom whispers to Becky, "You look incredible. I can't believe how lucky I am."

Becky whispers back, "You too, and me too."

The man behind the podium starts speaking, rings are exchanged, and before Becky knows, he has pronounced them husband and wife and, "You may kiss your bride". For just a second Becky panics, and thinks, "I've never kissed him. What if it's terrible?" But the kiss happens and it is wonderful. They turn to face the congregation and the pastor presents them as Mr. and Mrs. Watson. Becky's Mom gives her a puzzled look as the two walk down the aisle and out the door.

Everyone piles into their cars and head to El Casa Valdez restaurant for the reception. Becky and Tom are being driven over by one of Michael Dawn's limos, On the short drive over Tom comments, "What a story we are going to have to tell our kids."

Becky giggles and looks at Tom and says, "Just think, our first kiss was our wedding kiss."

"The first of many, many more to come," Tom says, and they kiss again.

When they come up for air Becky asks, "Tell me, who was the man that married us?"

"That was my Dad," Tom says as he jumps out of the Limo to run around and help his new bride out of the limousine, for they are now at the restaurant. "Come on, I'll introduce you." As he takes her hand, they are met by a man with a camera who says, "Come on, you guys, it's picture time," and herds the couple to a beautifully decorated room where the wedding party is gathered. Quick introductions are made as the photographer tells them where to stand and to smile. After about thirty minutes Mr. Valdez sticks his head in and says, "Hey guys, the food is getting cold and your guests are getting hungry, and they're anxious to congratulate the happy couple."

"Ok, we can take this out to the other room. I think I've got some good pictures from in here," the head photographer says. He happens to be from "The Zumiez Photography studio" which is owned by Blake and Tina Zumiez, one if the couples from church.

As Becky flutters around the large upstairs room meeting and greeting friends, family, and people she didn't know until today, she realizes how little she knows about the people in her church. She is surprised to learn that Tom's Dad, Mr. Larry Thomas Watson, is a pastor of a large church in the next state over, and that Tom is a third generation Sabbath keeping pastor. His grandfather on his Dad's side, Pastor Thomas Watson, had started a church and turned it over to his son when he retired. Tom was to take over, but decided to come to this town and start his own church. Besides this is where he could get a job as a male nurse. Tom has a much older brother, named Lawrence, who is 18 years older than Tom. Tom doesn't really know him very well because he is so much older than Tom. He knows his brother's daughter, Sara, who is only three years younger than Tom, much better since they are closer in age. She is the one Becky mistakenly thought was Tom's girlfriend.

She learns that Tom's mother, Candice Coolage-Watson, or CC, for short, is a retired office worker, as was her mother, Betty Jean Coolage who ran something called a comptometer. A pre-computer, calculator device. It wasn't even electric, all manual like her grandmother's typewriter. Becky can't even imagine such a thing.

Tom's parents had flown in for the wedding and were the special guests Pat had picked up from the airport.

As Becky rotates around the room, meeting and greeting people, she notices Tom talking to her parents. They seem to be getting along well. She wishes she knew what they were talking about.

After the reception Becky and her Mom find a restroom to get Becky changed and ready to go on her "honeymoon" mission trip that was to last anywhere from one to four years.

"That Tom of yours makes a lot of sense. I think your Dad and I are going to start going to that church of yours," Mrs. Kelsey Watson Becky's mom says.

"Mom, that is terrific. I've been praying for that," Becky says.

"Well, I'm not promising anything, but we will go check it out," her mom says.

"That's all I ask," Becky says, as she hugs her mom.

"I can't believe you are going away for four years. I'm going to miss you so much."

"Mom, I'll miss you too. And I promise to contact you whenever I can. Besides it might not last for four years. It could end in as little as one year," Becky says.

"That's still a long time, and if I know you, you'll be there for the full four," her Mom says.

Becky changes into a new white pants suit that her mom gives her as a going away present. Her mom looks at her daughter and says, "You are so beautiful, I can't believe you are married and leaving. It's all so sudden," as she fights back the tears. "I'm very proud of you."

"Thanks mom, and don't cry or you will get me crying too," Becky says as they both laugh, which is a release in itself.

"I can't believe I'm married and going on a mission trip to who knows where. Are you sure this is all real or am I dreaming?" Becky asks her mom.

"I wish, but no, it's all real. You better get going. You don't want to keep your new husband waiting, who just happens to have the same last name as you. Are you sure you're not related?" Her now composed mom says as she ushers her daughter out the door.

Becky looks at her mom with a shocked look and says, "Mom, I didn't think of that. Do you think that's possible?"

Clara, who accidently overhears the last of the conversation, reassures them both by saying, "Don't worry. I checked both of your lineages and I can assure you you're not related."

Both Becky and her mom give a sigh of relief.

They meet Tom, who has also changed clothes, and Becky takes his arm as they head to the waiting limo amongst the rice and bubbles that rain down on them as they make their way through the crowd. The limo is decorated with the usual "just married" graffiti. The limo takes them to a hotel across from the airport. As they get out Becky starts panicking and says, "I never had time to pack, I have no clothes!"

The driver calmly tells her, "It's ok, madam, your friends and your mother packed these two suitcases for you and this carry on. And your friends packed these two for you, Mr. Tom, plus this carry on."

Tom and Becky look at the brand new suitcases packed in the trunk of the large car. Two are pink and two are dark blue. The driver, a Mr. Jim Baldwyn, takes the cases out of the trunk and piles them onto the sidewalk, gets back in the car and pulls away. A doorman is immediately there helping them with their bags and escorting them to the check in desk. The hotel is a five star upscale place. Becky looks at Tom and asks, "Can we afford this place?" as the desk clerk asks, "Name, please?" Tom tells him, "Mr. and Mrs. Tom

Watson." The clerk says, "Yes, I have you right here. You're in the honeymoon suite. You are all paid up for the night."

Tom looks at Becky and says, "I guess we can afford this place. It must be the church's wedding present to us."

"We have a very generous church, who loves you very much," Becky says.

"They love both of us. And you are right, they are a great bunch of people," Tom says smiling. "Shall we go to our room, Mrs. Watson?"

Becky replies, "Yes, we shall, Mr. Watson." They walk arm in arm to their room.

"Tomorrow morning we board a plane, heading for the rest of our lives together," Tom says as he picks up his new bride and carries her over the threshold of their room.

The End

Post Script

Almost four years later Lisa's letter finally catches up to Becky and Tom.

Dear Becky, and Tom,

I hope this letter finds you, and that you are both alive and well.

I have so much to tell you. It's been three years since you left and a lot has happened.

First I will tell you about work. Soon after you left, Mr. James had a small heart attack and decided it was time to sell the business and get out. He did admit it was a mistake to have fired you. Three families from church went in together and bought the business and put me in charge of the whole thing. I fired Scott and hired Veronica full time. Things have been going well since then. The business is thriving. I'm still learning things about running a thriving business. It's all very exciting. I love going to work now. I think I have made it fun for all of the employees as well, at least as fun as possible.

I will tell you that as soon as you guys get home, you have a guaranteed job as my head assistant, waiting for you with an equally generous salary I might add, if you want it, of course.

Next, your mom and dad have been coming to church when they are in town, but I will let them tell you about what's happening with them, when you see them again.

The sad news is Ms. Marcie Carcie passed away one week after her 100th birthday. She died in her sleep, very peacefully. The town gave her a huge birthday party with a parade and everything. Very exciting. I hope it wasn't too much for her. She left everything she had to the church, which ended up being quite a large sum of money.

Pat had a lot of good ideas on how to get the word out that we are here. As a result we have grown by leaps and bounds. One of Mr. James' holdings was that huge abandoned hotel on the out skirts of town close the fairgrounds called "The Oases". When the group at church bought out Mr. James they got the hotel as well. They donated the smaller of the two towers to the church. We all got together and fixed it up. Crystal is a natural interior decorator. It has a restaurant with a large kitchen, for making and eating all of our meals together. Crystal runs the kitchen and is our head chef. The church tower has an indoor heated pool and separate hot tub. We can use either one for baptisms. These are both just off the lobby behind a glass wall. So no more boiling water on the stove to heat up the horse trough, yeah! People will take advantage of the pool and hot tub during our breaks in the service and during the week as well. The teenagers love it and will sometimes hold an informal class in the pool or hot tub. The church has enough rooms on the first floor for all of the Sabbath school rooms we need. There's a big meeting room which we use as our main sanctuary. The people that have to travel to get here all have a permanent room or suite to come stay in from Friday night to Sunday morning, as most of these people do stay until Sunday. (They are free to use their rooms whenever they want for as long as they want.) On Friday before sundown we clean and get all the food ready as much as we can. Then on Sunday we clean things again before leaving for our homes. Crystal runs the restaurant during the week, Monday - Thursday. It's very popular. It's simply called 'The Vegetarian.' Crystal, Jeff and their daughter Wendy live at the church in a three bedroom suite behind the restaurant. Jeff is the church's manager / treasurer and oversees the business end of the church. Martha and Clara are joint head housekeepers. We have 100 rooms or suits in the church tower part of the hotel. Most of the rooms are claimed by permanent church members. The other rooms we use for visiting speakers or for church goers that happen to be passing through. We usually have a full house. Tom will have a hay day keeping up with all the landscaping (Ha Ha). The church claims one acre of the total of the hotels land which is extensive. There are flower gardens and walking trails throughout all of the grounds. The hotel sets on the bank of the river and has a marvelous view. There is also an outdoor theater for putting on plays. Next door there is a horse camp with bunk houses and cabins, and some horses and ponies that we can ride or just enjoy watching from the veranda, and there is a watch donkey that brays her head off if there is an intruder. We have use of this as a kids camp during the summer and we also use it as a feast site for Tabernacles. The main hotel is still called "The Oasis." We added "The Lord of The Sabbath, Oasis" to our part of the hotel. Mr. Valdez has a second restaurant in the "big tower" which is the main part of the actual hotel. The "El

Casa Valdez 2". Rachel and her mom run it together. It also is very popular. The whole thing has truly been a generous gift from God.

Rachel had a big healthy baby boy who they named Roger Patrick Abbot. She got so big everyone thought she was going to have twins. He weighed over 11 pounds at birth, and was 25 inches long.

Crystal on the other hand, hardy even looked pregnant. Her daughter, Wendy, has a rare condition called 'extreme dwarfism'. She is in the 'Guinness Book of Records' as the smallest full term baby ever. She only weighed 8 ounces, and was 4 inches long. You could literally hold her in the palm of your hand. Crystal dresses her in doll clothes because that is all she can find that will fit her. Other than being extremely small she is quite healthy. Now at the age of 26 months, she weighs a whopping 1 pound and stands 5 inches tall. She is so cute. She is the pride of the town. All the girls in the church just love her and think of her as a living doll. Unfortunately Wendy does have to be closely monitored by her doctors, which gets expensive, so the church has adopted them and we cover all of their doctor bills and give them a free place to live, plus a salary for all the work Jeff does managing the church.

Roger on the other hand is huge. At the same age as little Wendy he is more than twelve times as big as she is. He weighs in at a healthy 60 pounds and is almost three feet tall. He looks like a football player. To see Wendy and Roger together is really something. Of course we are extra careful when the two of them are together. Roger could really hurt Wendy without even trying. But he is very careful around her and protects her like a big brother. Both moms are good moms and very attentive to their children's needs. Wendy also has a Pomeranian dog named Daisy that stays by her side 24-7. She is a small dog to us, but to Wendy she is a horse. Ha ha. Daisy pulls a Wendy-sized cart around that Wendy rides in. Wendy can walk but she gets tired quickly and often rides in the cart. Daisy is quick to let you know she is there, so that no one steps on them. Daisy also makes a fuss if Wendy needs anything. Wendy's voice is so high and small it's easy to miss it, but you can't miss Daisy. Daisy even wears one of those service dog coats so she can go where other dogs can't.

Remember the pastor from the Baptist church that verbally attacked you at the store? Well, he came to the church just long enough to learn about the Sabbath and then went back to his church and changed it over to a Sabbath keeping church. It's now a Seventh Day Baptist church. Though I don't think they keep the Holy Days, at least not yet, but Crystal is working on him. He wants to apologize to you for jumping all over you. He said he was being bothered by the Holy Spirit to change to a Sabbath keeper but was resisting it. Then you and Crystal changed and it hit a cord. He reacted in the wrong way. He has since turned from his evil ways and fully embraces God and the whole Bible, mostly, anyway. He said he was sorry and thanks you and Crystal for being the catalyst for turning him around. The Bible and the truth has really taken off since we had that revival, the one I didn't tell you about. That was one of Pat's ideas. Almost everyone in this town keeps the Sabbath and most keep the Holy Days too. Even the restaurants stopped serving pork or any other unclean thing and close for the Sabbath and the Holy Days. It's amazing how much love is in this town now. Just walking down the street you can feel the love. Everyone says "Hi" and "Can I help you with anything". It's a different town from the one you left three years ago. I guess you will be coming home in another year. I suspect Roger will be four feet tall by then and Wendy might be a whole 5 1/2 inches tall. She only grows about a half inch a year.

I can hardly wait to see the two of you again. I really miss you both. There is so much more I want to tell you, but if I try to write it all down in this letter it will turn into a book.

Love in Christ
Lisa, and family.

About the Author

Debbie J. Libbey is a wife and mother who has gone to many churches and denominations searching for the truth. She has put her ideal church into this book. She has written other books and poems but this is her first to get published. With hopes of publishing others.

Debbie also loves animals and is a semi-retired Laboratory Animal Technician.